THE PRISON-SHIP ADVENTURE OF JAMES FORTEN,

REVOLUTIONARY WAR CAPTIVE

BY *MARTY RHODES FIGLEY*

ADAPTATION BY **AMANDA DOERING TOURVILLE**

ILLUSTRATED BY **TED HAMMOND** *AND* **RICHARD PIMENTEL CARBAJAL**

Graphic Universe™ Minneapolis

INTRODUCTION

JAMES FORTEN WAS BORN ON SEPTEMBER 2, 1766, IN PHILADELPHIA, PENNSYLVANIA. PHILADELPHIA WAS THE LARGEST CITY IN THE AMERICAN COLONIES. JAMES'S PARENTS WERE FREE AFRICAN AMERICANS, BUT HIS GRANDPARENTS HAD BEEN SLAVES.

JAMES'S FATHER WAS A SAILMAKER. AS A YOUNG BOY, JAMES WENT TO WORK WITH HIS FATHER, LEARNING TO MAKE SAILS. WHEN JAMES WAS SEVEN YEARS OLD, HIS FATHER DIED. FOR A FEW YEARS, JAMES WENT TO A QUAKER SCHOOL. HE LEARNED TO READ AND TO WORK WITH NUMBERS. BUT HIS FAMILY NEEDED MONEY, SO JAMES TOOK A JOB IN A STORE. JAMES GAVE THE MONEY HE EARNED TO HIS FAMILY.

AT THIS TIME, GREAT BRITAIN RULED THE COLONIES. BUT BY THE 1770S, THE COLONISTS WANTED THEIR FREEDOM. IN 1776, THE LEADERS OF THE

AMERICAN COLONIES SIGNED THE DECLARATION OF INDEPENDENCE. THIS DOCUMENT SAID THAT AMERICA WAS A NEW COUNTRY FREE FROM GREAT BRITAIN. JAMES JOINED THE CROWD IN PHILADELPHIA TO HEAR THE DECLARATION READ TO THE PUBLIC FOR THE FIRST TIME. BUT AMERICA WOULD STILL HAVE TO FIGHT GREAT BRITAIN FOR ITS INDEPENDENCE.

JAMES WANTED TO DO HIS PART TO HELP AMERICA WIN ITS FREEDOM. HE WENT TO SEA ON THE *ROYAL LOUIS*, A PRIVATELY OWNED SHIP THAT HELPED THE AMERICAN CAUSE. HIS JOB WAS TO BRING GUNPOWDER TO THE SHIP'S CANNONS. HIS DESIRE TO HELP WAS ABOUT TO BE TESTED.

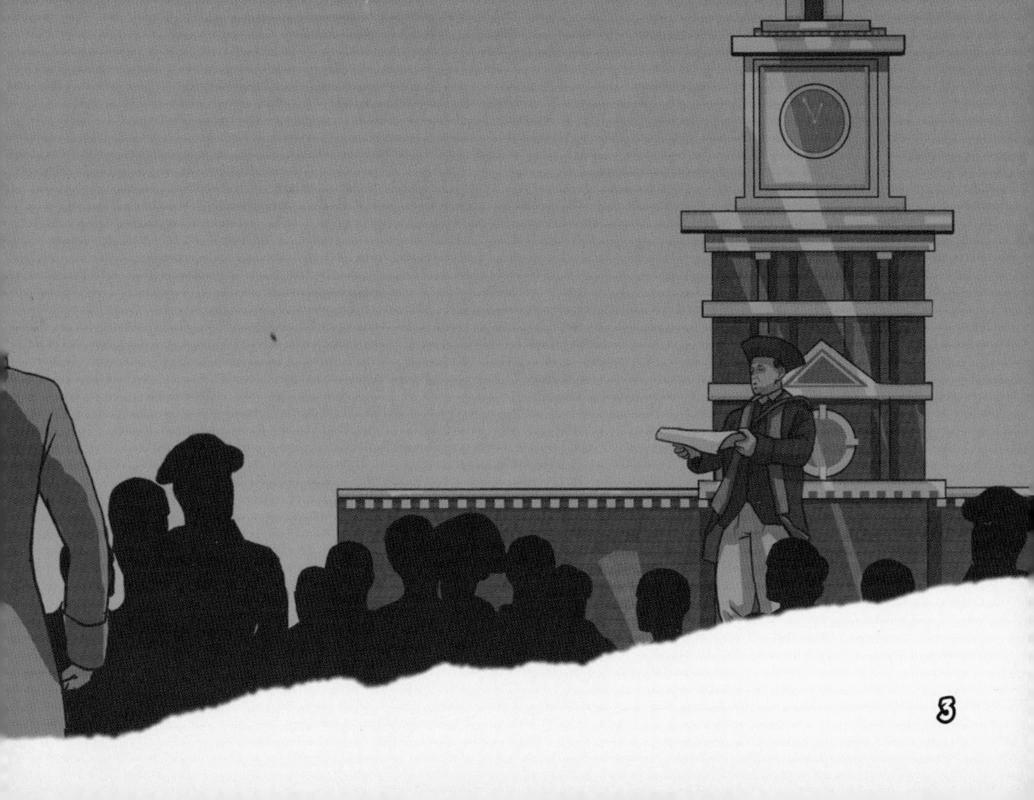

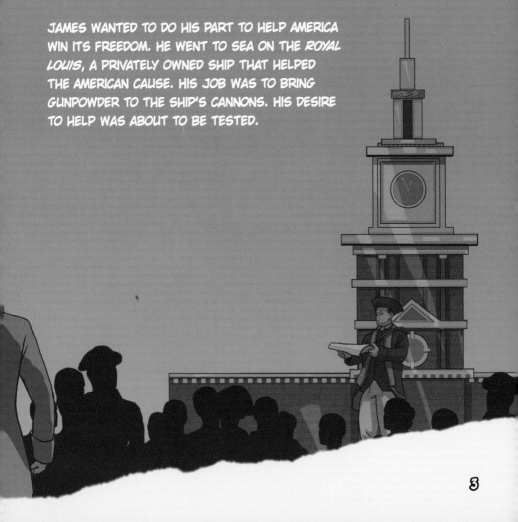

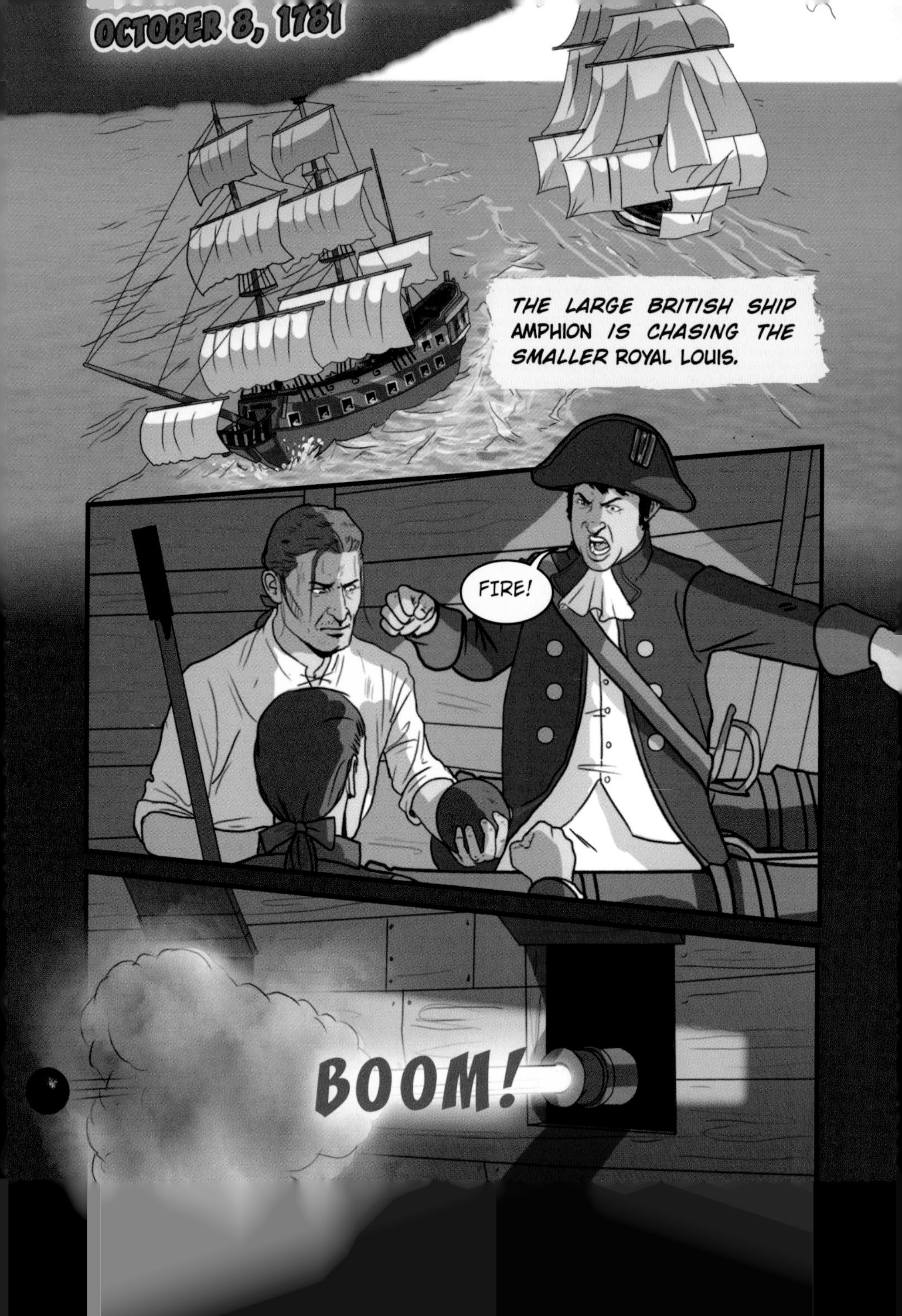
OCTOBER 8, 1781
THE LARGE BRITISH SHIP AMPHION IS CHASING THE SMALLER ROYAL LOUIS.
FIRE!
BOOM!

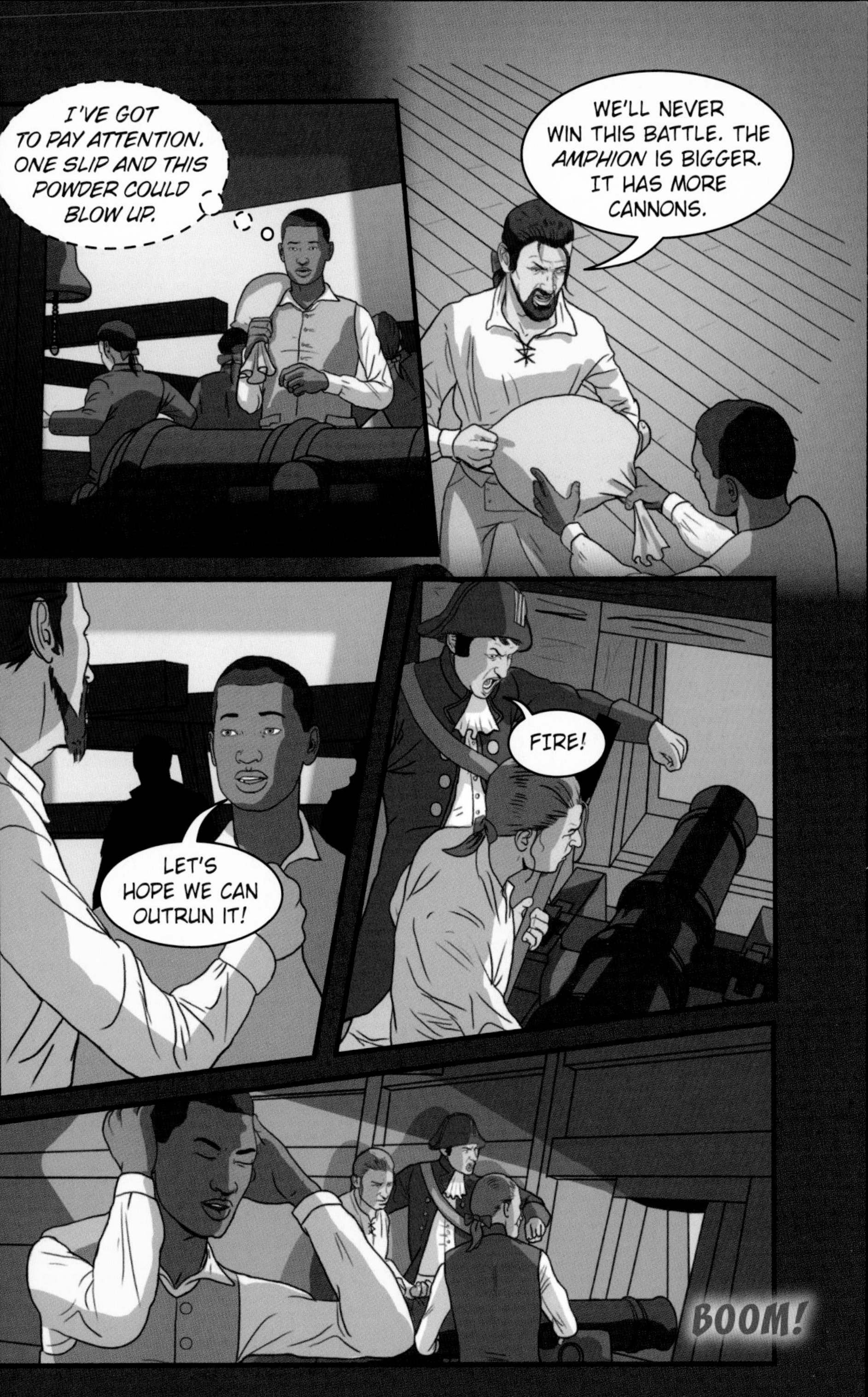
I'VE GOT TO PAY ATTENTION. ONE SLIP AND THIS POWDER COULD BLOW UP.
WE'LL NEVER WIN THIS BATTLE. THE *AMPHION* IS BIGGER. IT HAS MORE CANNONS.
LET'S HOPE WE CAN OUTRUN IT!
FIRE!
BOOM!

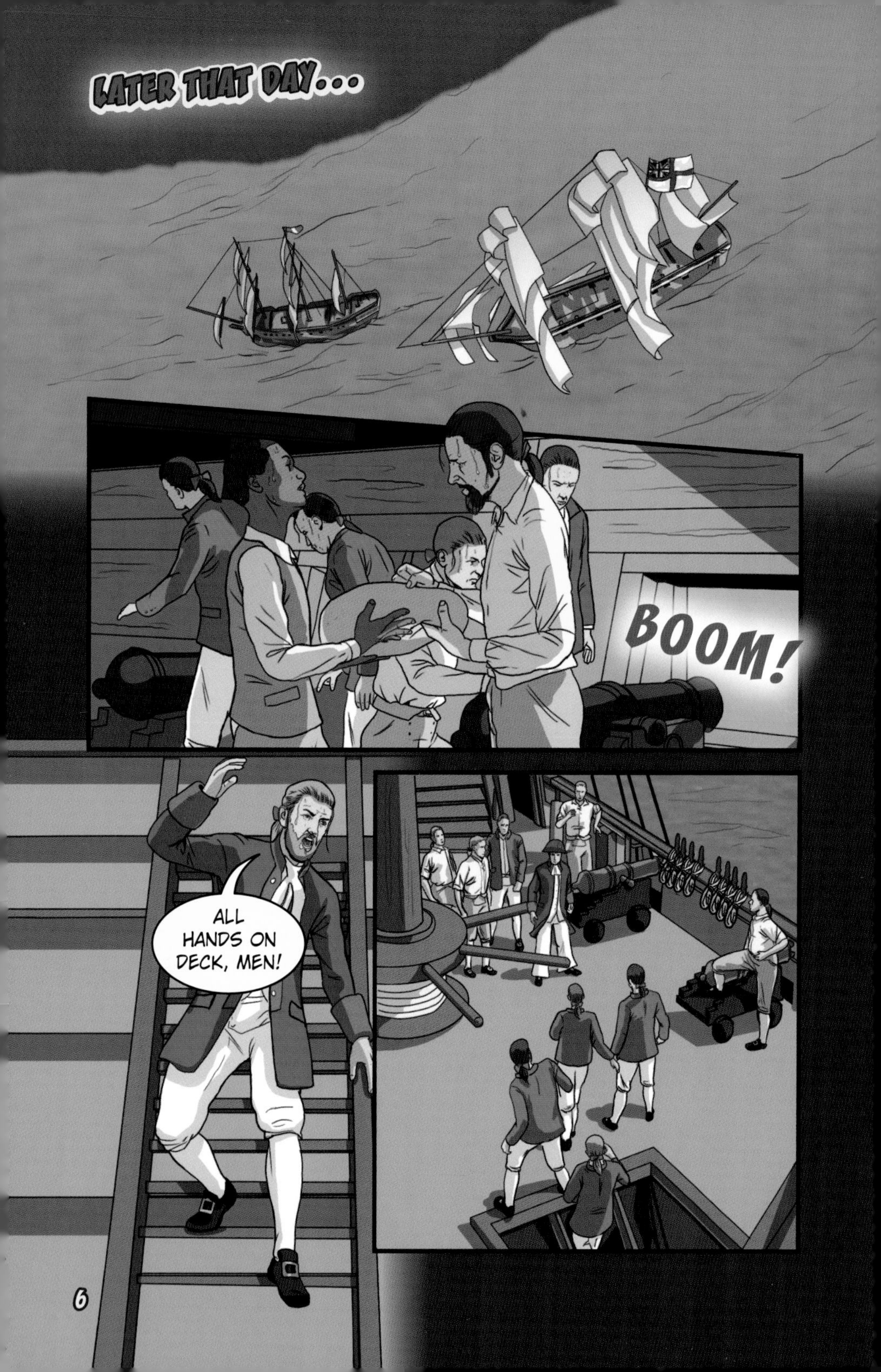
LATER THAT DAY...
BOOM!
ALL HANDS ON DECK, MEN!

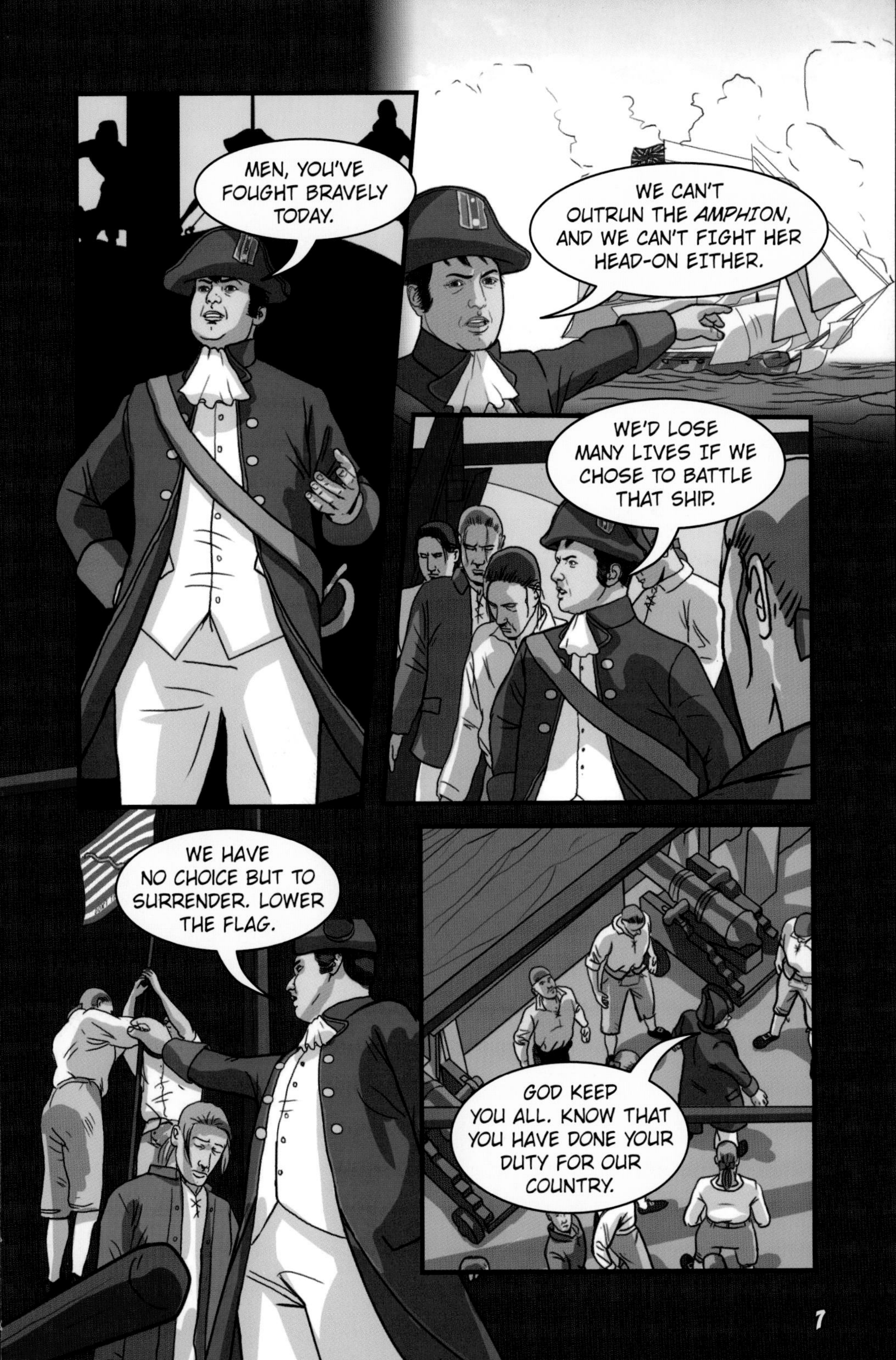
MEN, YOU'VE FOUGHT BRAVELY TODAY.
WE CAN'T OUTRUN THE *AMPHION*, AND WE CAN'T FIGHT HER HEAD-ON EITHER.
WE'D LOSE MANY LIVES IF WE CHOSE TO BATTLE THAT SHIP.
WE HAVE NO CHOICE BUT TO SURRENDER. LOWER THE FLAG.
GOD KEEP YOU ALL. KNOW THAT YOU HAVE DONE YOUR DUTY FOR OUR COUNTRY.

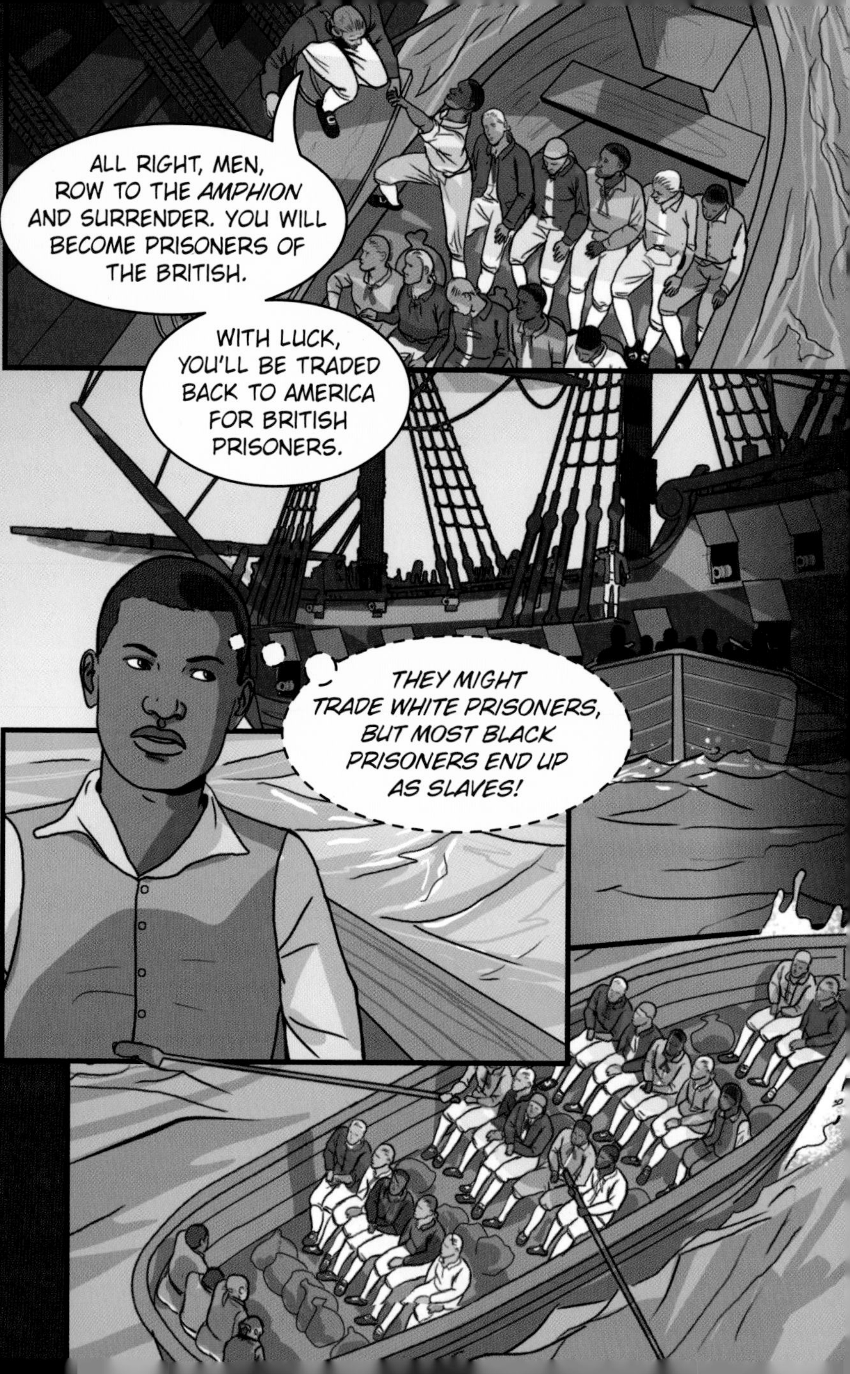
ALL RIGHT, MEN, ROW TO THE *AMPHION* AND SURRENDER. YOU WILL BECOME PRISONERS OF THE BRITISH.
WITH LUCK, YOU'LL BE TRADED BACK TO AMERICA FOR BRITISH PRISONERS.
THEY MIGHT TRADE WHITE PRISONERS, BUT MOST BLACK PRISONERS END UP AS SLAVES!

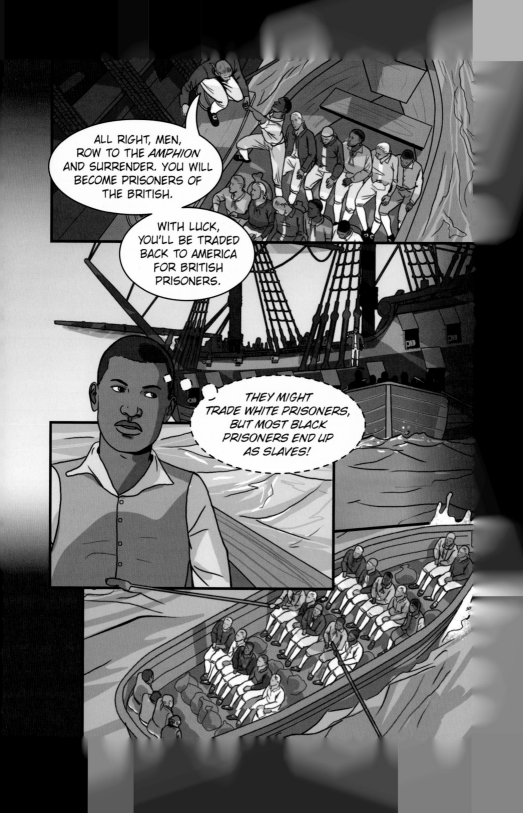

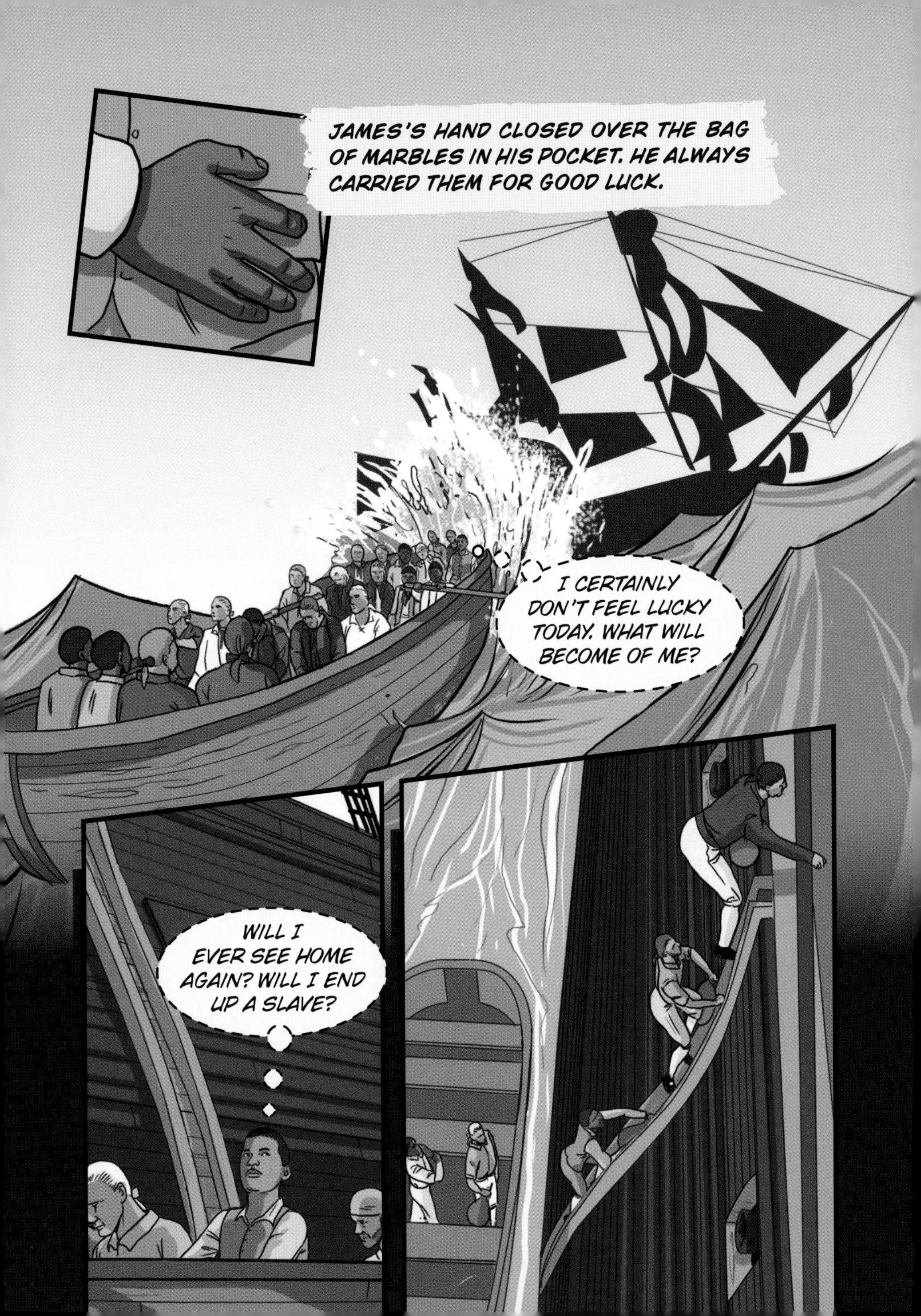
JAMES'S HAND CLOSED OVER THE BAG OF MARBLES IN HIS POCKET. HE ALWAYS CARRIED THEM FOR GOOD LUCK.
I CERTAINLY DON'T FEEL LUCKY TODAY. WHAT WILL BECOME OF ME?
WILL I EVER SEE HOME AGAIN? WILL I END UP A SLAVE?

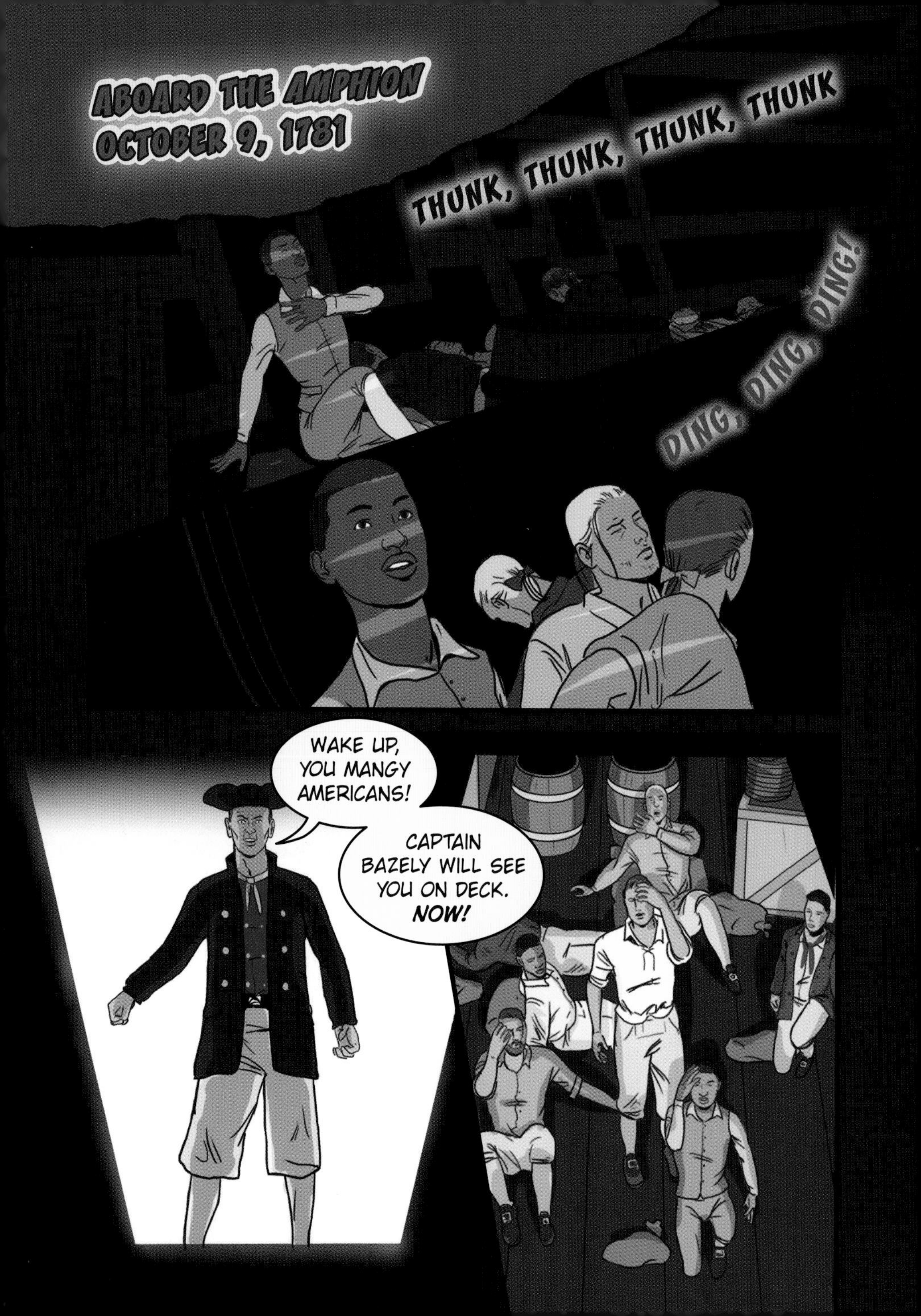
ABOARD THE AMPHION
OCTOBER 9, 1781
THUNK, THUNK, THUNK, THUNK
DING, DING, DING!
WAKE UP, YOU MANGY AMERICANS!
CAPTAIN BAZELY WILL SEE YOU ON DECK. NOW!

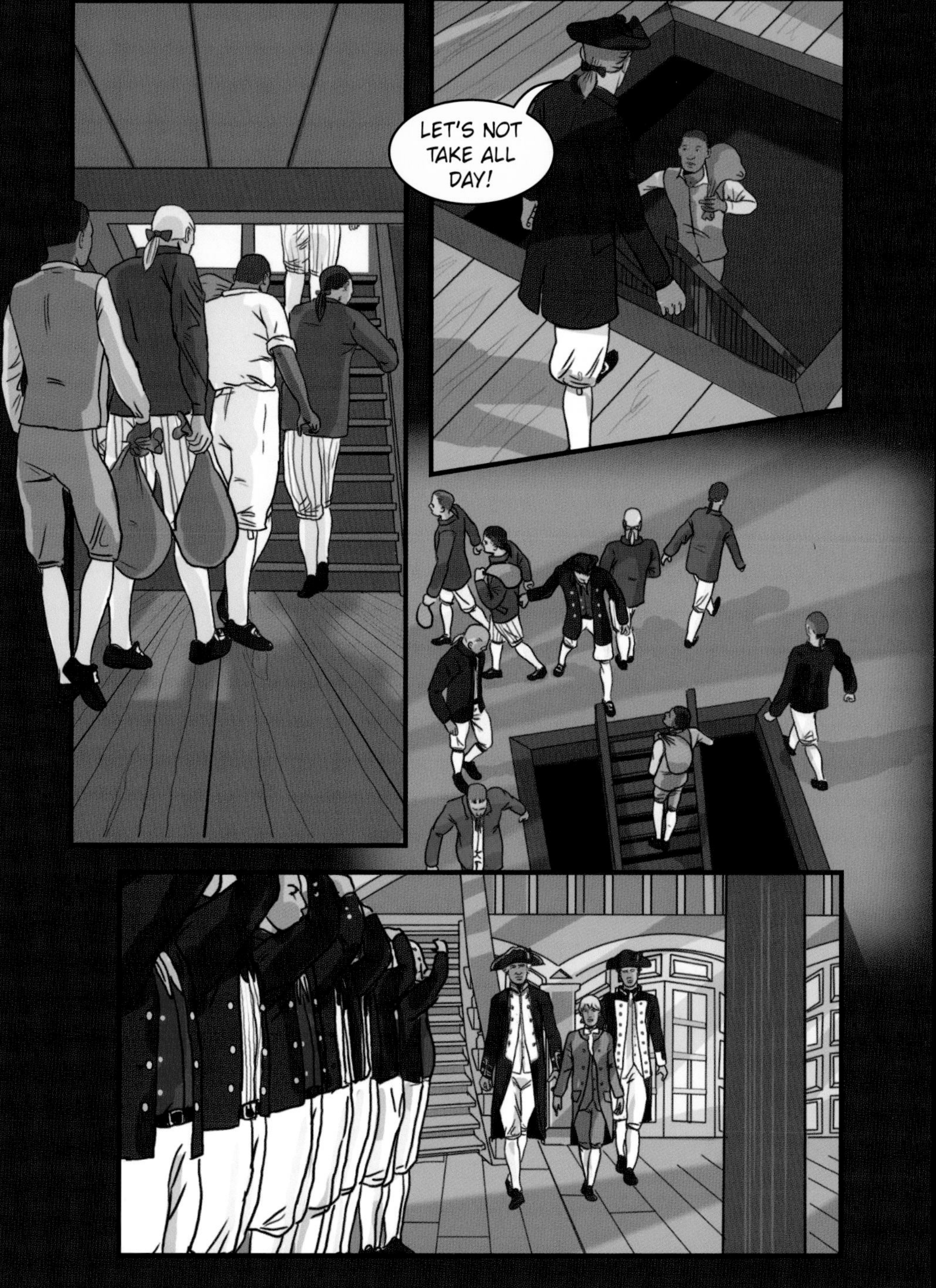
LET'S NOT TAKE ALL DAY!

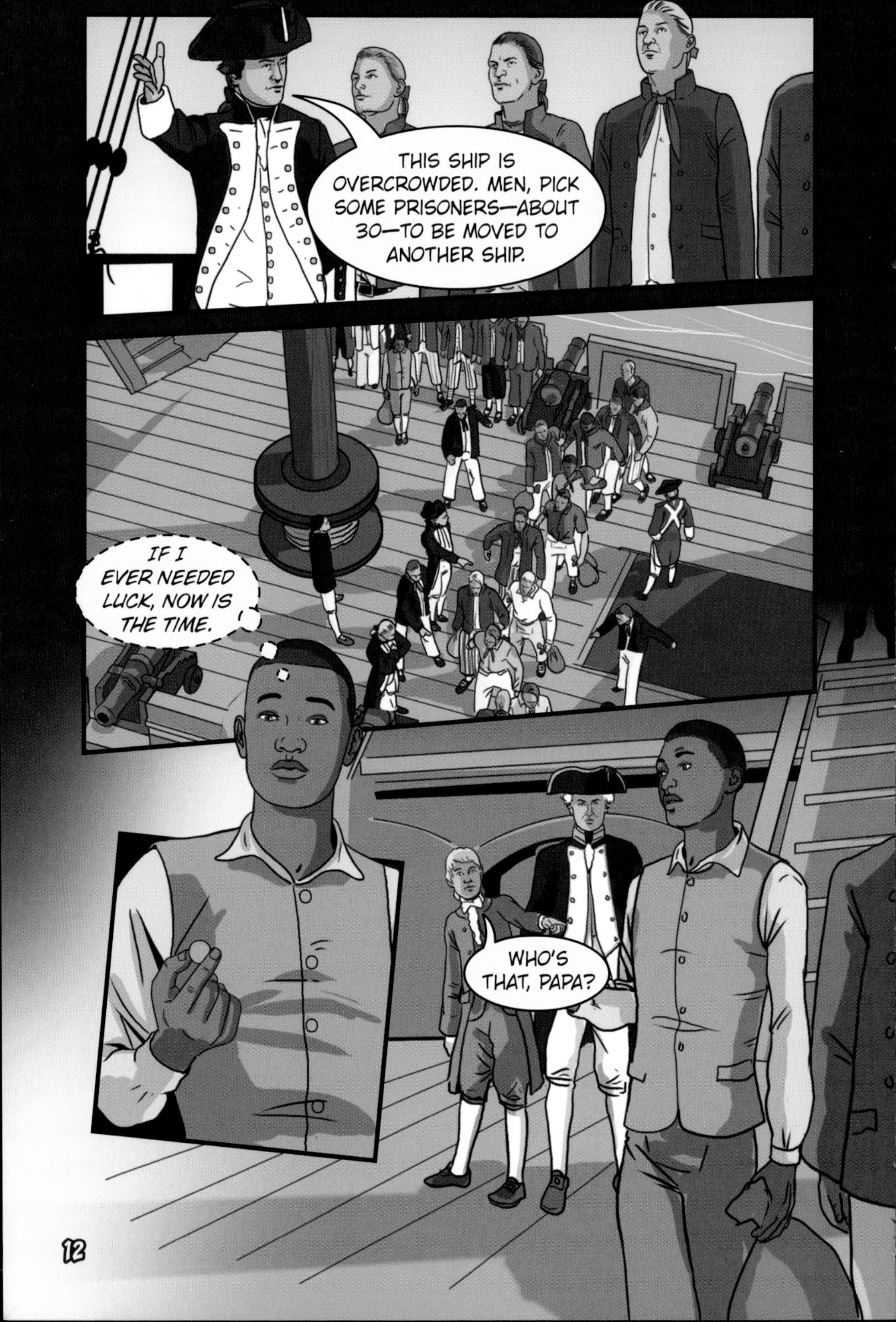
THIS SHIP IS OVERCROWDED. MEN, PICK SOME PRISONERS—ABOUT 30—TO BE MOVED TO ANOTHER SHIP.
IF I EVER NEEDED LUCK, NOW IS THE TIME.
WHO'S THAT, PAPA?

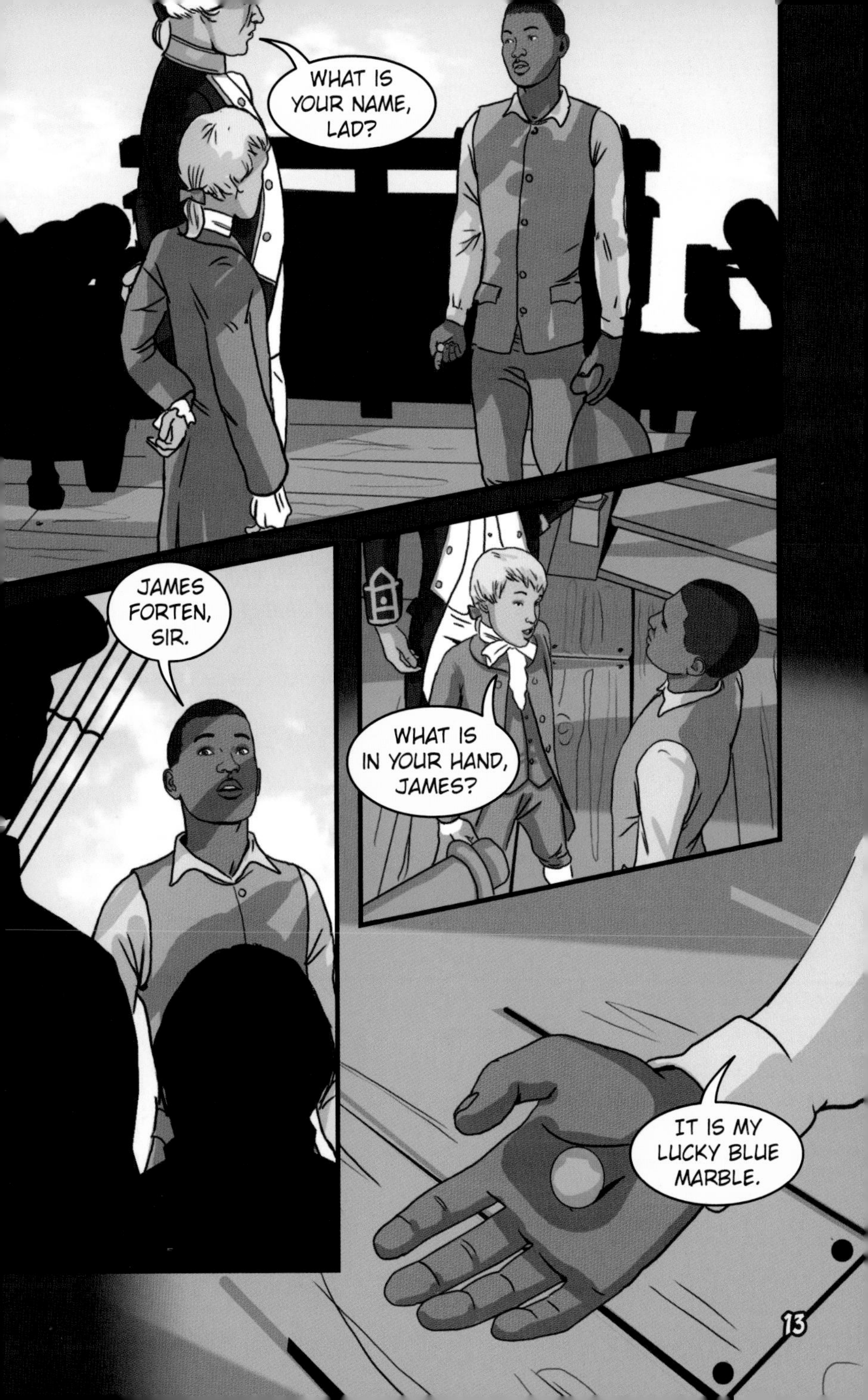
WHAT IS YOUR NAME, LAD?
JAMES FORTEN, SIR.
WHAT IS IN YOUR HAND, JAMES?
IT IS MY LUCKY BLUE MARBLE.

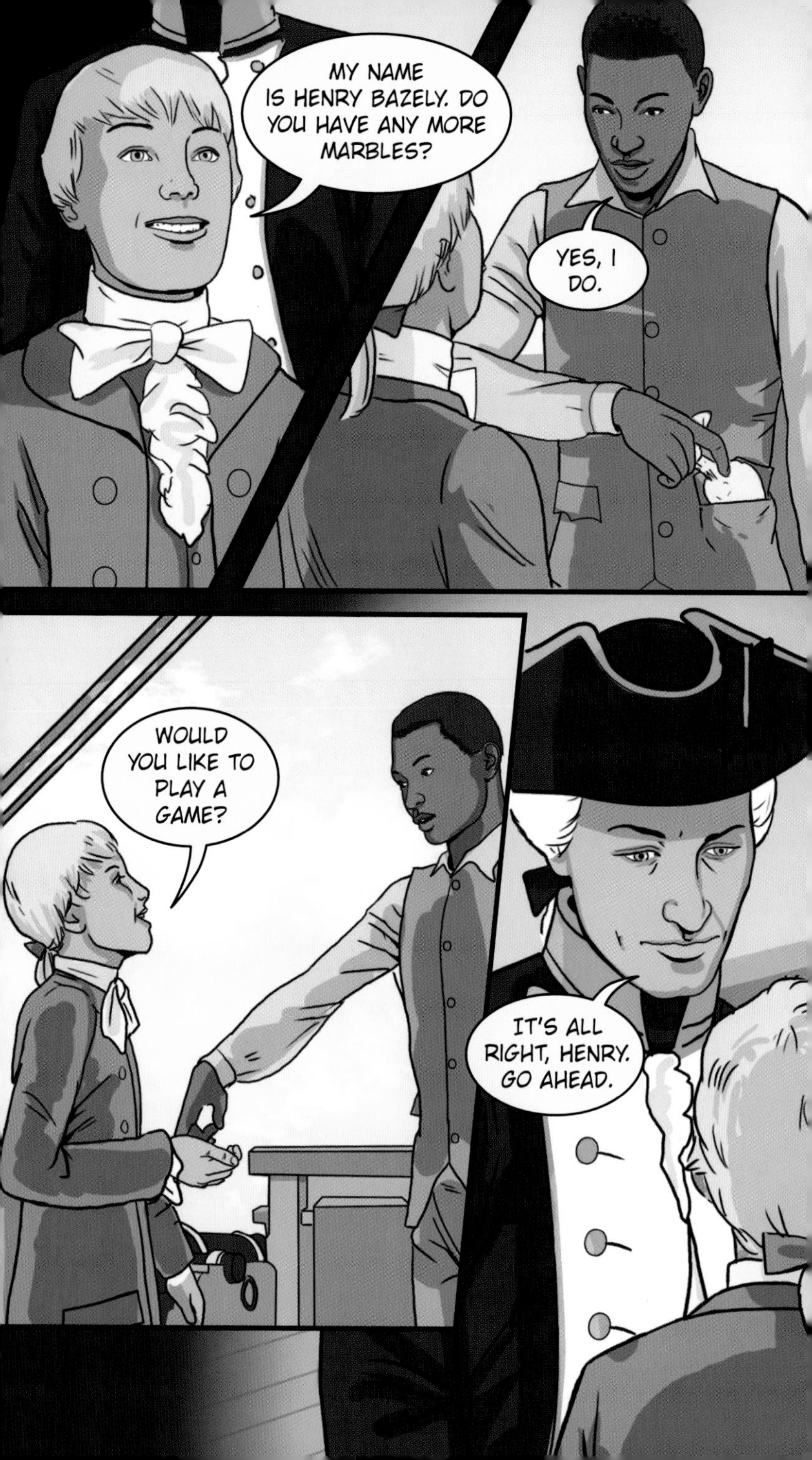
MY NAME IS HENRY BAZELY. DO YOU HAVE ANY MORE MARBLES?
YES, I DO.
WOULD YOU LIKE TO PLAY A GAME?
IT'S ALL RIGHT, HENRY. GO AHEAD.

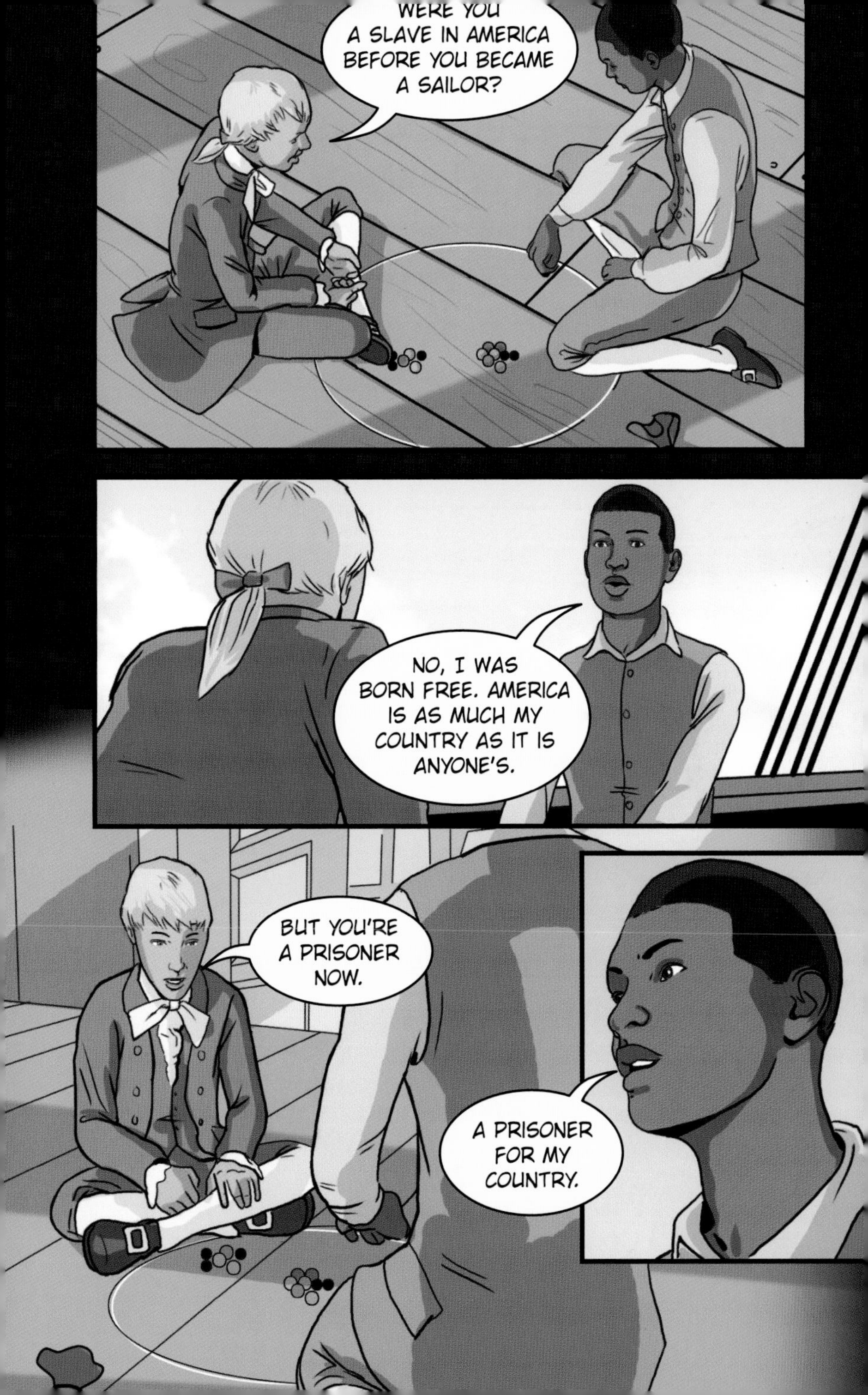
WERE YOU A SLAVE IN AMERICA BEFORE YOU BECAME A SAILOR?
NO, I WAS BORN FREE. AMERICA IS AS MUCH MY COUNTRY AS IT IS ANYONE'S.
BUT YOU'RE A PRISONER NOW.
A PRISONER FOR MY COUNTRY.

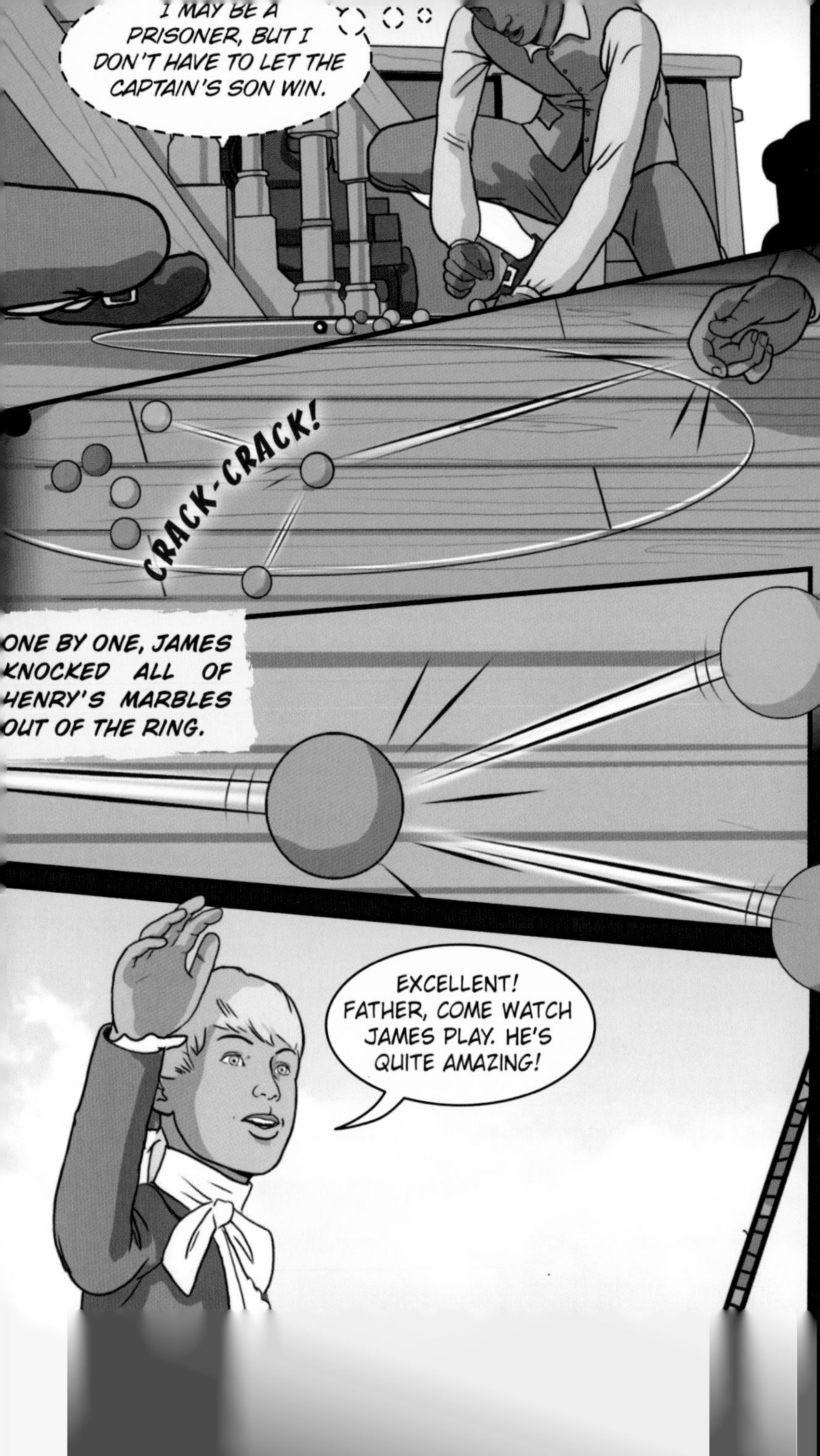
I MAY BE A PRISONER, BUT I DON'T HAVE TO LET THE CAPTAIN'S SON WIN.
CRACK-CRACK!
ONE BY ONE, JAMES KNOCKED ALL OF HENRY'S MARBLES OUT OF THE RING.
EXCELLENT! FATHER, COME WATCH JAMES PLAY. HE'S QUITE AMAZING!

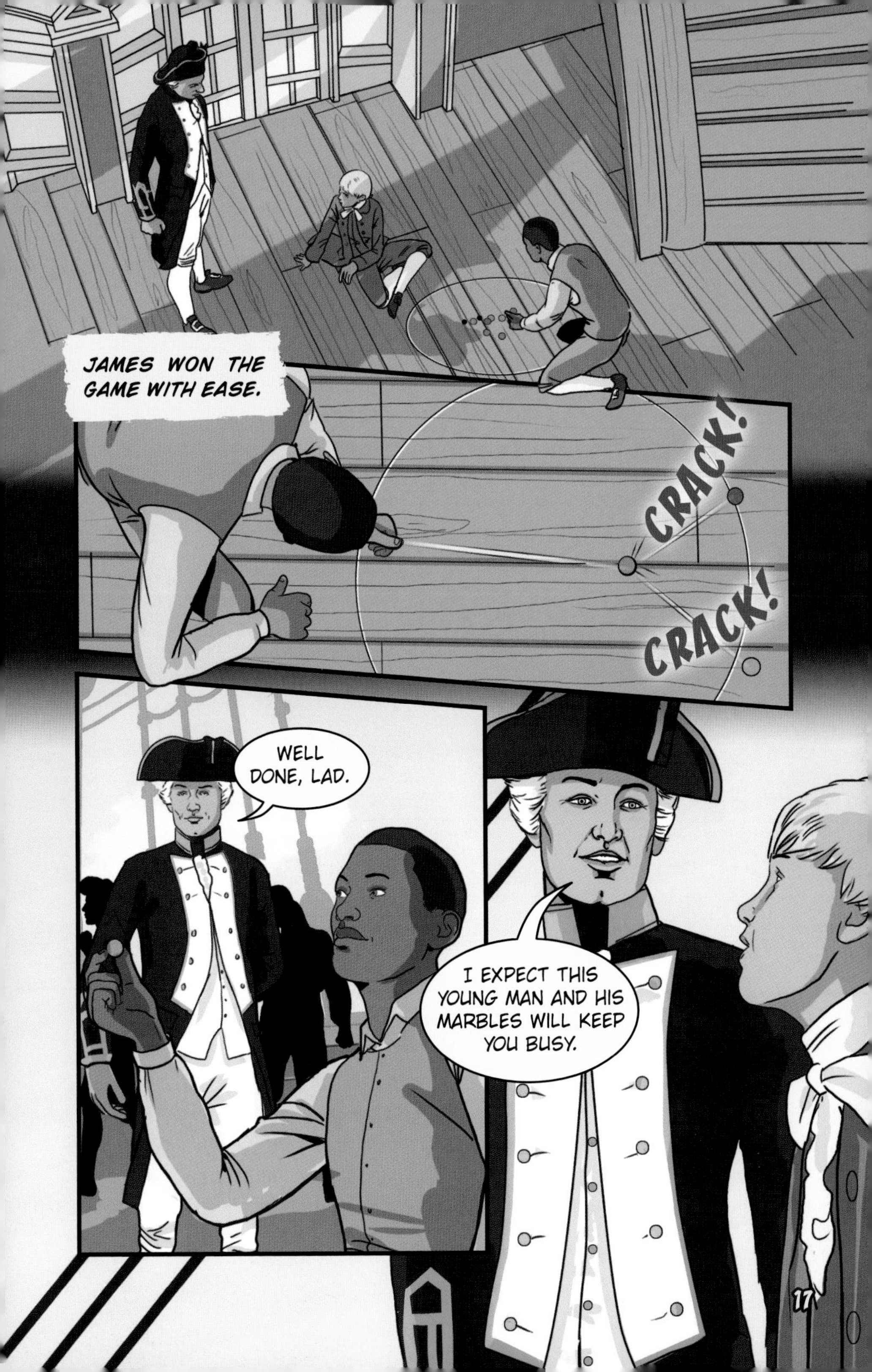
JAMES WON THE GAME WITH EASE.
CRACK!
CRACK!
WELL DONE, LAD.
I EXPECT THIS YOUNG MAN AND HIS MARBLES WILL KEEP YOU BUSY.

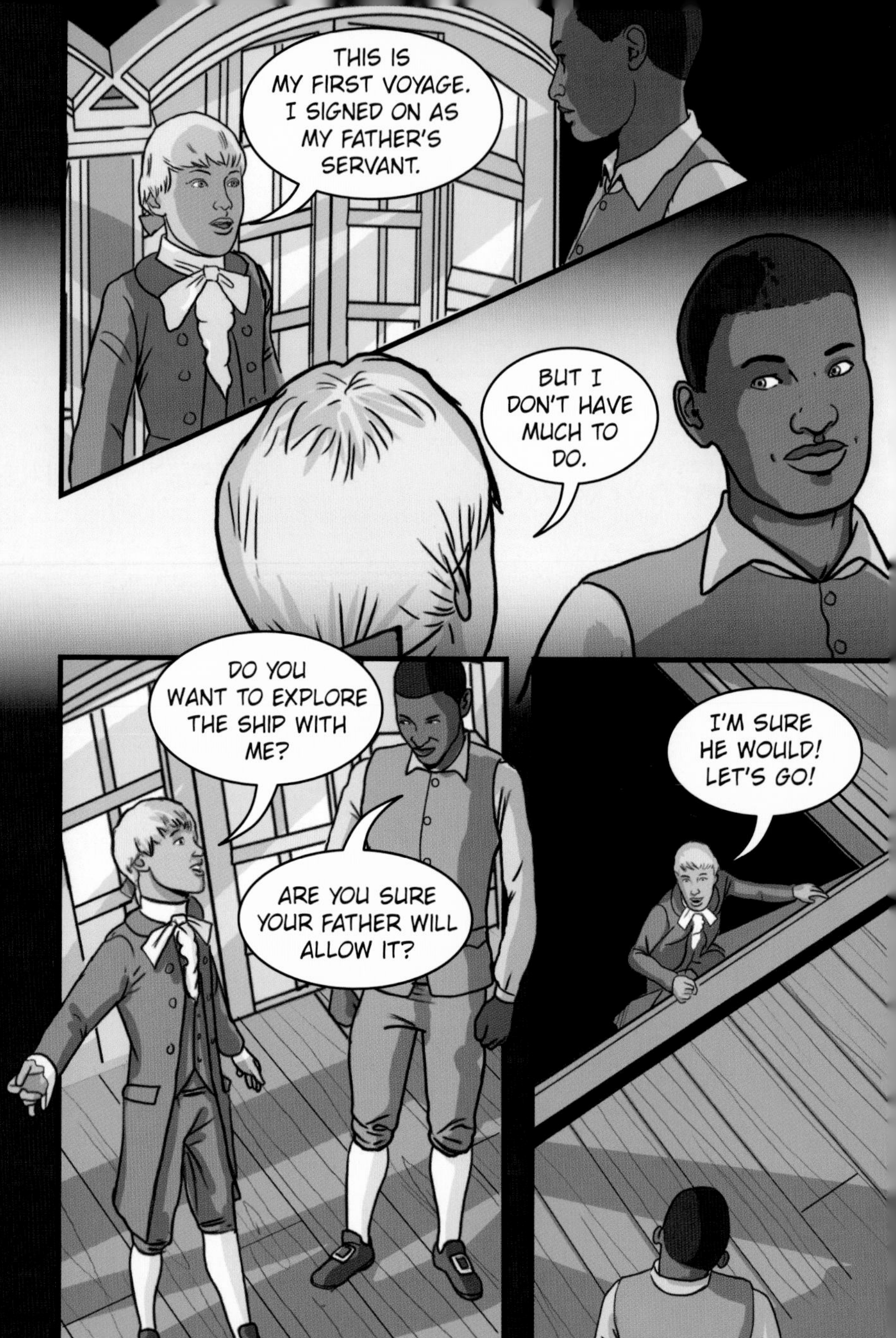
THIS IS MY FIRST VOYAGE. I SIGNED ON AS MY FATHER'S SERVANT.
BUT I DON'T HAVE MUCH TO DO.
DO YOU WANT TO EXPLORE THE SHIP WITH ME?
ARE YOU SURE YOUR FATHER WILL ALLOW IT?
I'M SURE HE WOULD! LET'S GO!

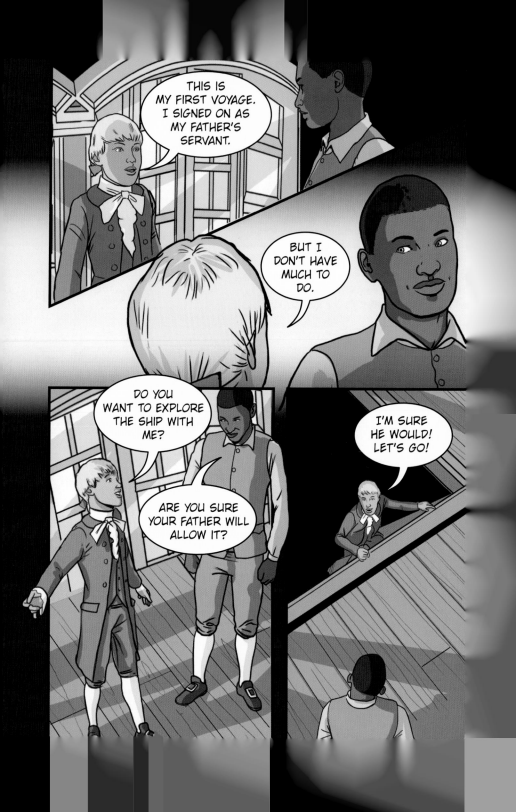

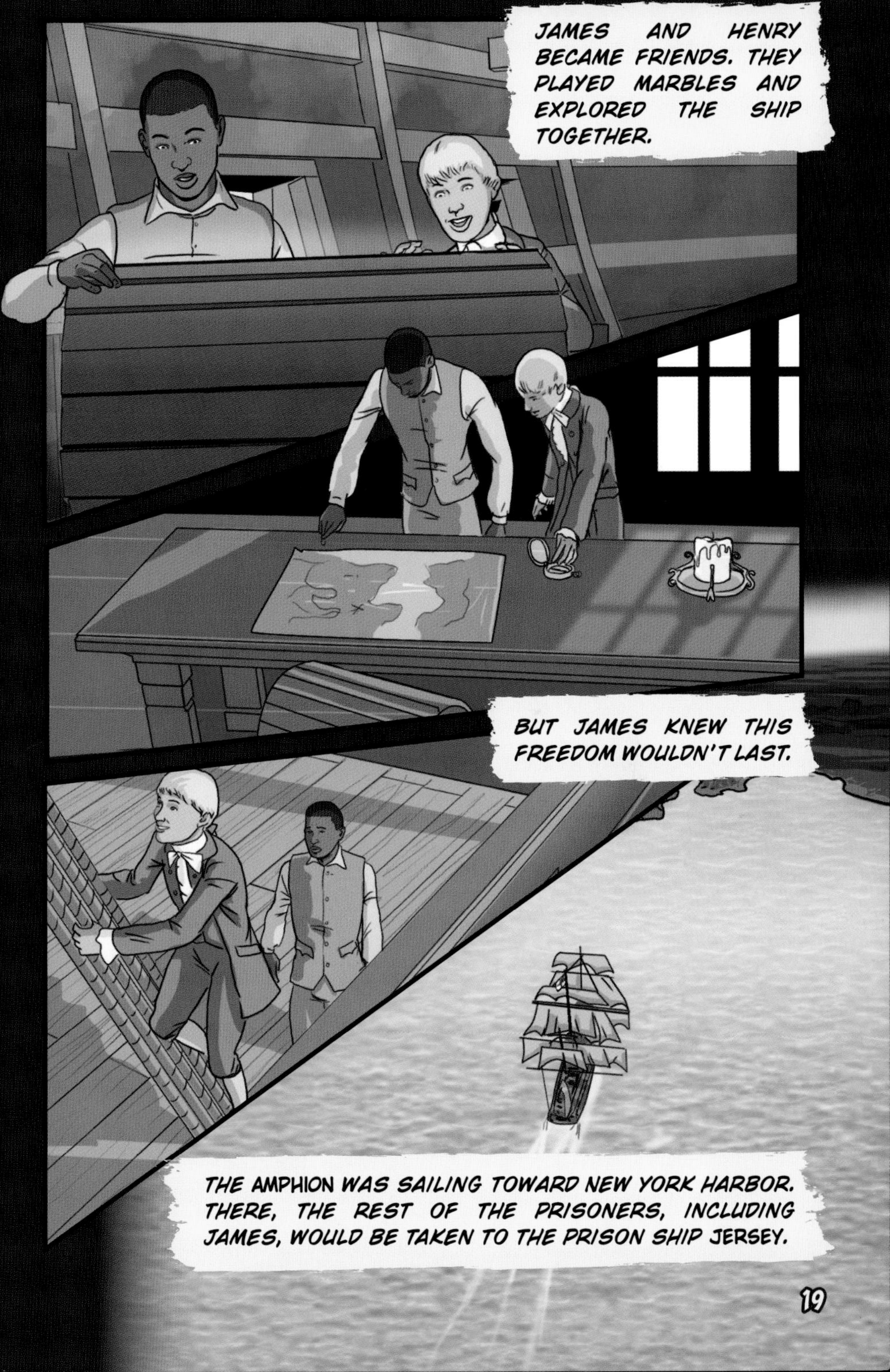
JAMES AND HENRY BECAME FRIENDS. THEY PLAYED MARBLES AND EXPLORED THE SHIP TOGETHER.
BUT JAMES KNEW THIS FREEDOM WOULDN'T LAST.
THE AMPHION WAS SAILING TOWARD NEW YORK HARBOR. THERE, THE REST OF THE PRISONERS, INCLUDING JAMES, WOULD BE TAKEN TO THE PRISON SHIP JERSEY.

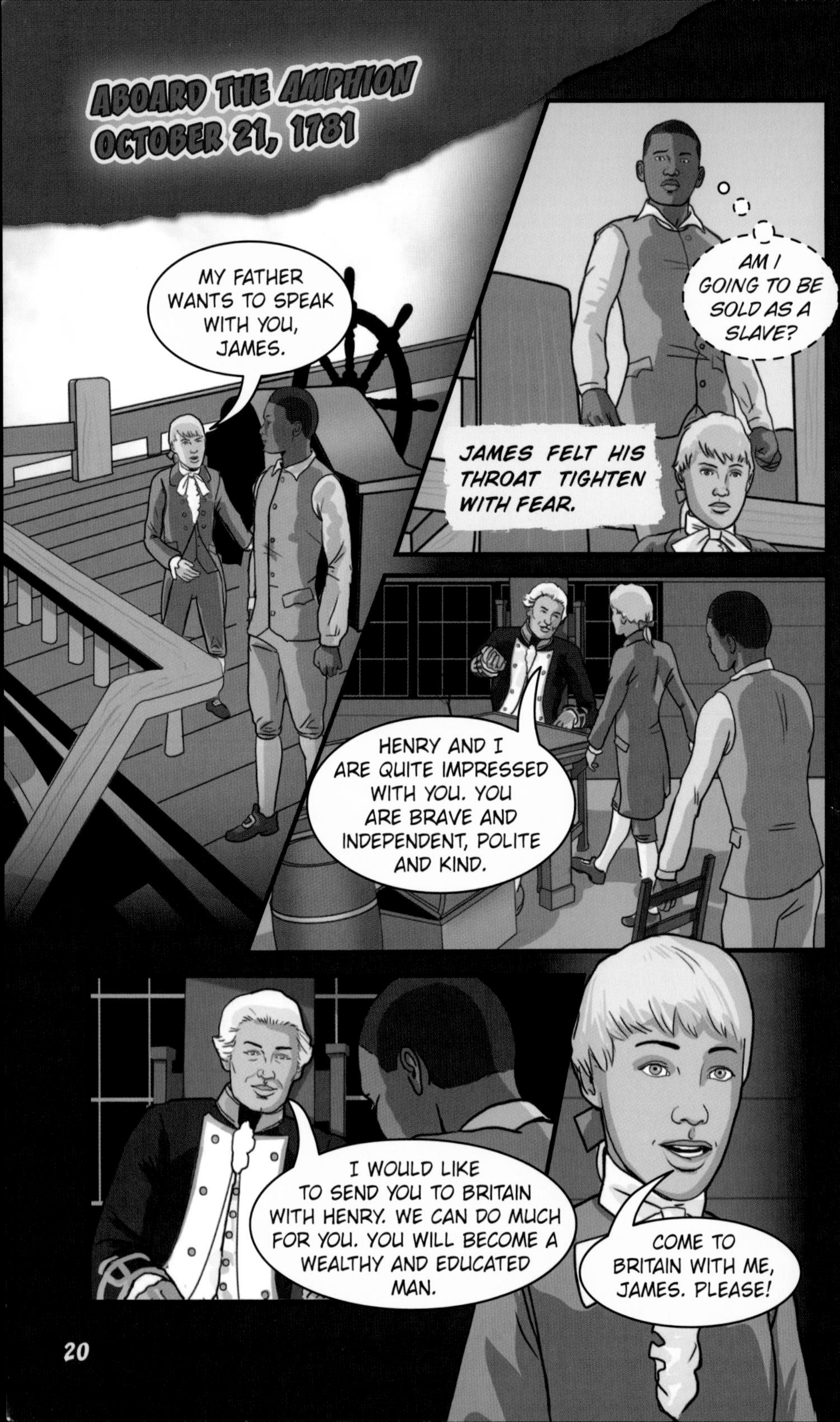
ABOARD THE AMPHION
OCTOBER 21, 1781
MY FATHER WANTS TO SPEAK WITH YOU, JAMES.
AM I GOING TO BE SOLD AS A SLAVE?
JAMES FELT HIS THROAT TIGHTEN WITH FEAR.
HENRY AND I ARE QUITE IMPRESSED WITH YOU. YOU ARE BRAVE AND INDEPENDENT, POLITE AND KIND.
I WOULD LIKE TO SEND YOU TO BRITAIN WITH HENRY. WE CAN DO MUCH FOR YOU. YOU WILL BECOME A WEALTHY AND EDUCATED MAN.
COME TO BRITAIN WITH ME, JAMES. PLEASE!

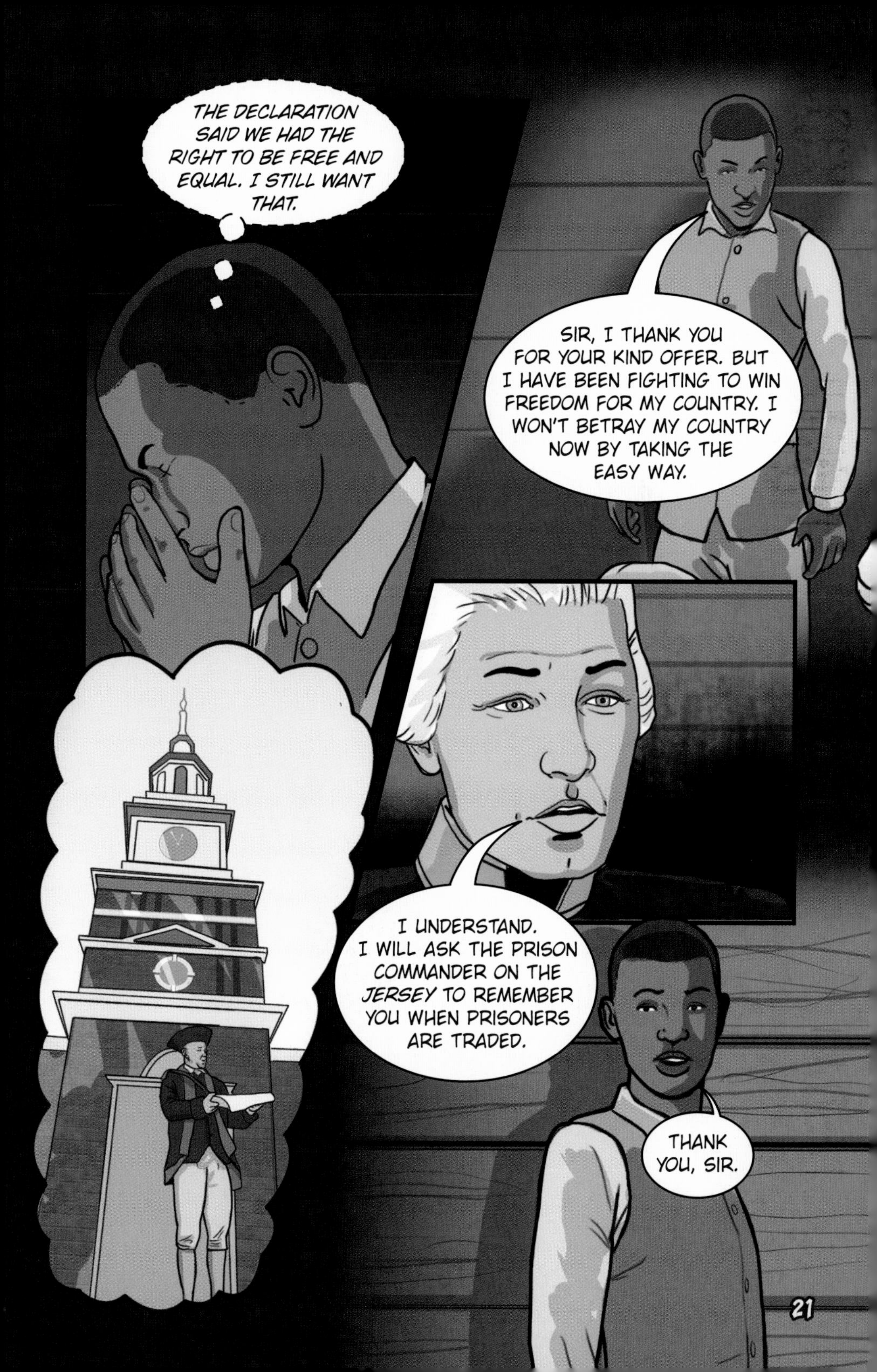
THE DECLARATION SAID WE HAD THE RIGHT TO BE FREE AND EQUAL. I STILL WANT THAT.
SIR, I THANK YOU FOR YOUR KIND OFFER. BUT I HAVE BEEN FIGHTING TO WIN FREEDOM FOR MY COUNTRY. I WON'T BETRAY MY COUNTRY NOW BY TAKING THE EASY WAY.
I UNDERSTAND. I WILL ASK THE PRISON COMMANDER ON THE *JERSEY* TO REMEMBER YOU WHEN PRISONERS ARE TRADED.
THANK YOU, SIR.

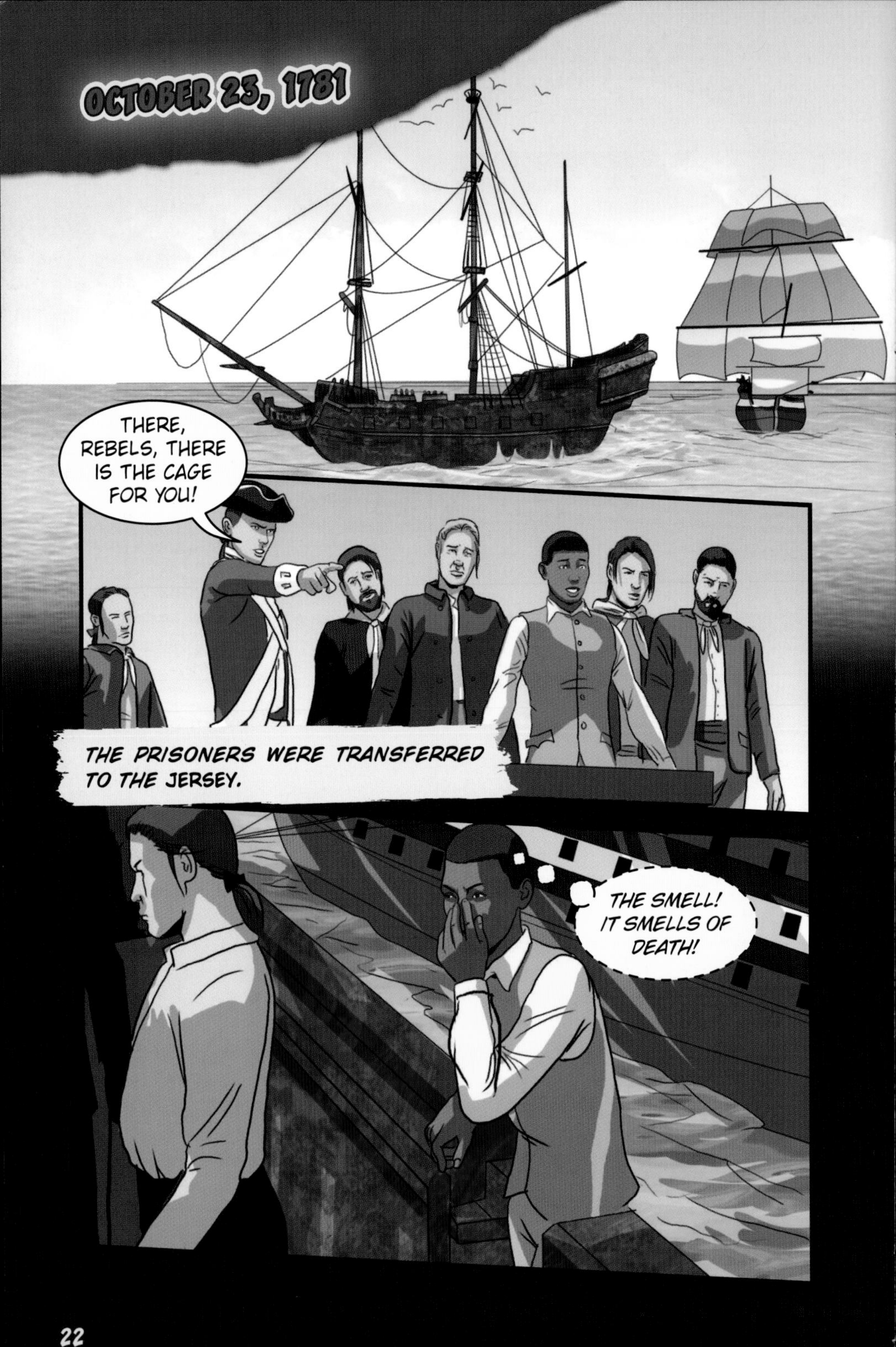
OCTOBER 23, 1781
THERE, REBELS, THERE IS THE CAGE FOR YOU!
THE PRISONERS WERE TRANSFERRED TO THE JERSEY.
THE SMELL! IT SMELLS OF DEATH!

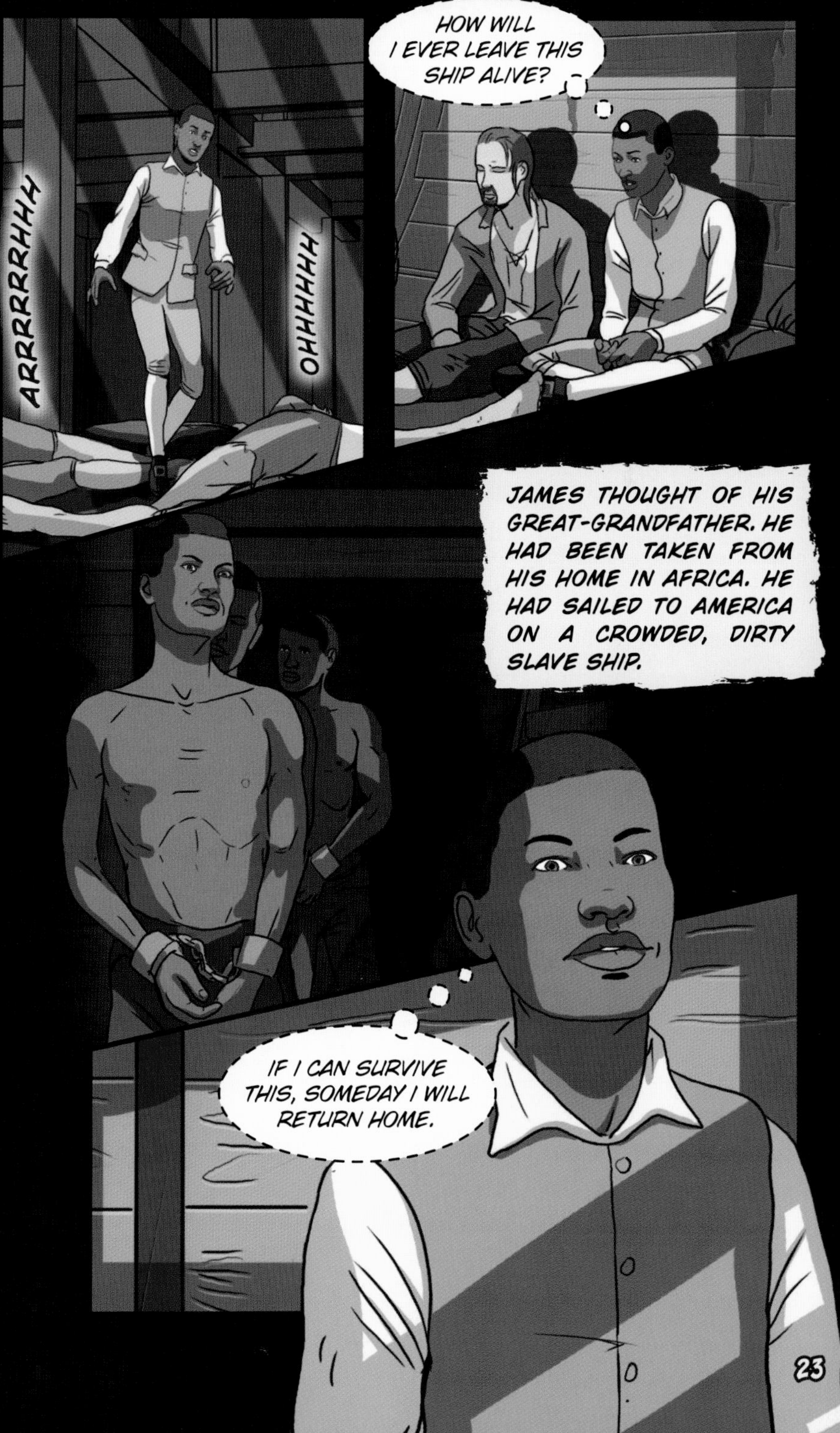
ARRRRRRHHH
OHHHHHH
HOW WILL I EVER LEAVE THIS SHIP ALIVE?
JAMES THOUGHT OF HIS GREAT-GRANDFATHER. HE HAD BEEN TAKEN FROM HIS HOME IN AFRICA. HE HAD SAILED TO AMERICA ON A CROWDED, DIRTY SLAVE SHIP.
IF I CAN SURVIVE THIS, SOMEDAY I WILL RETURN HOME.

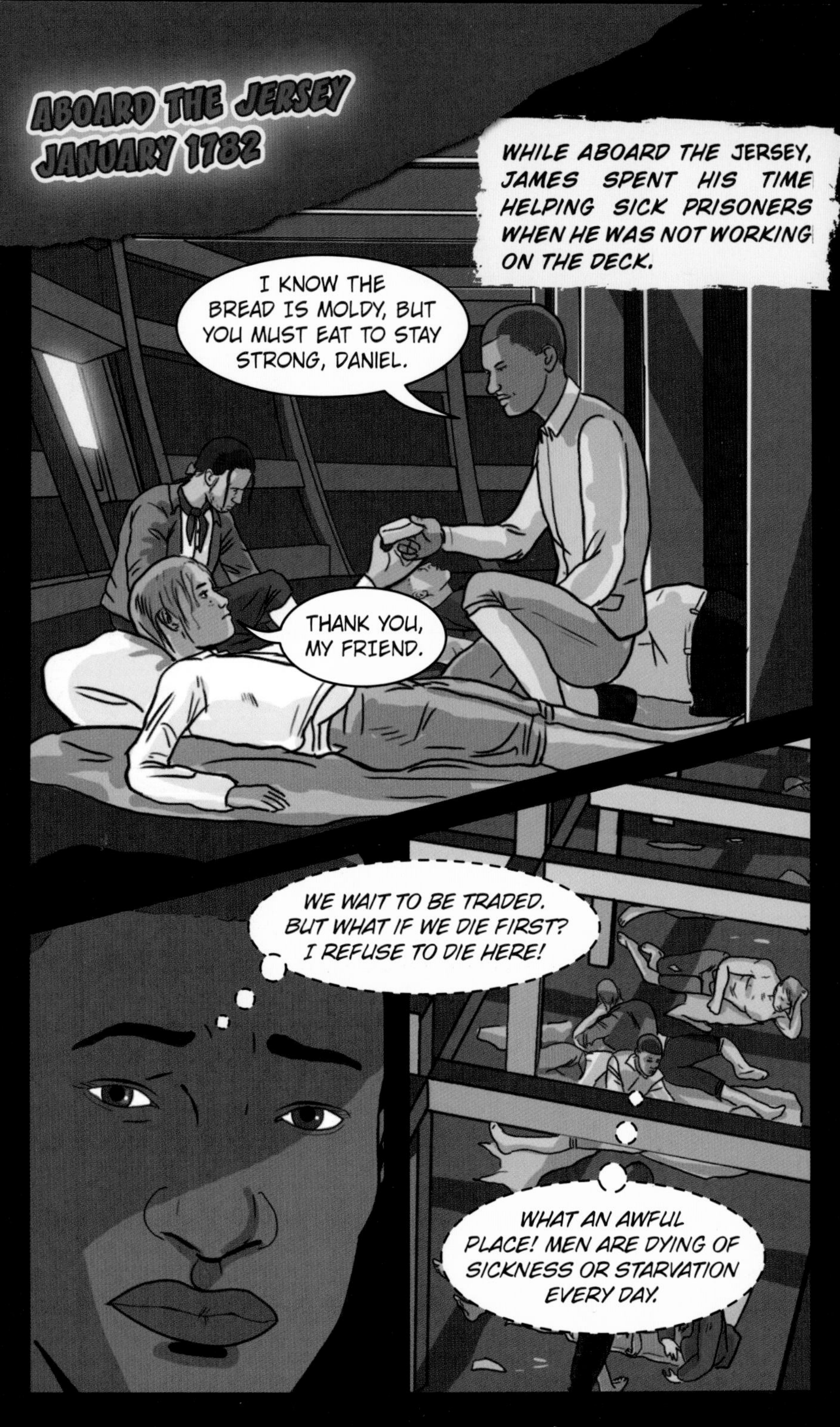
ABOARD THE JERSEY JANUARY 1782
WHILE ABOARD THE JERSEY, JAMES SPENT HIS TIME HELPING SICK PRISONERS WHEN HE WAS NOT WORKING ON THE DECK.
I KNOW THE BREAD IS MOLDY, BUT YOU MUST EAT TO STAY STRONG, DANIEL.
THANK YOU, MY FRIEND.
WE WAIT TO BE TRADED. BUT WHAT IF WE DIE FIRST? I REFUSE TO DIE HERE!
WHAT AN AWFUL PLACE! MEN ARE DYING OF SICKNESS OR STARVATION EVERY DAY.

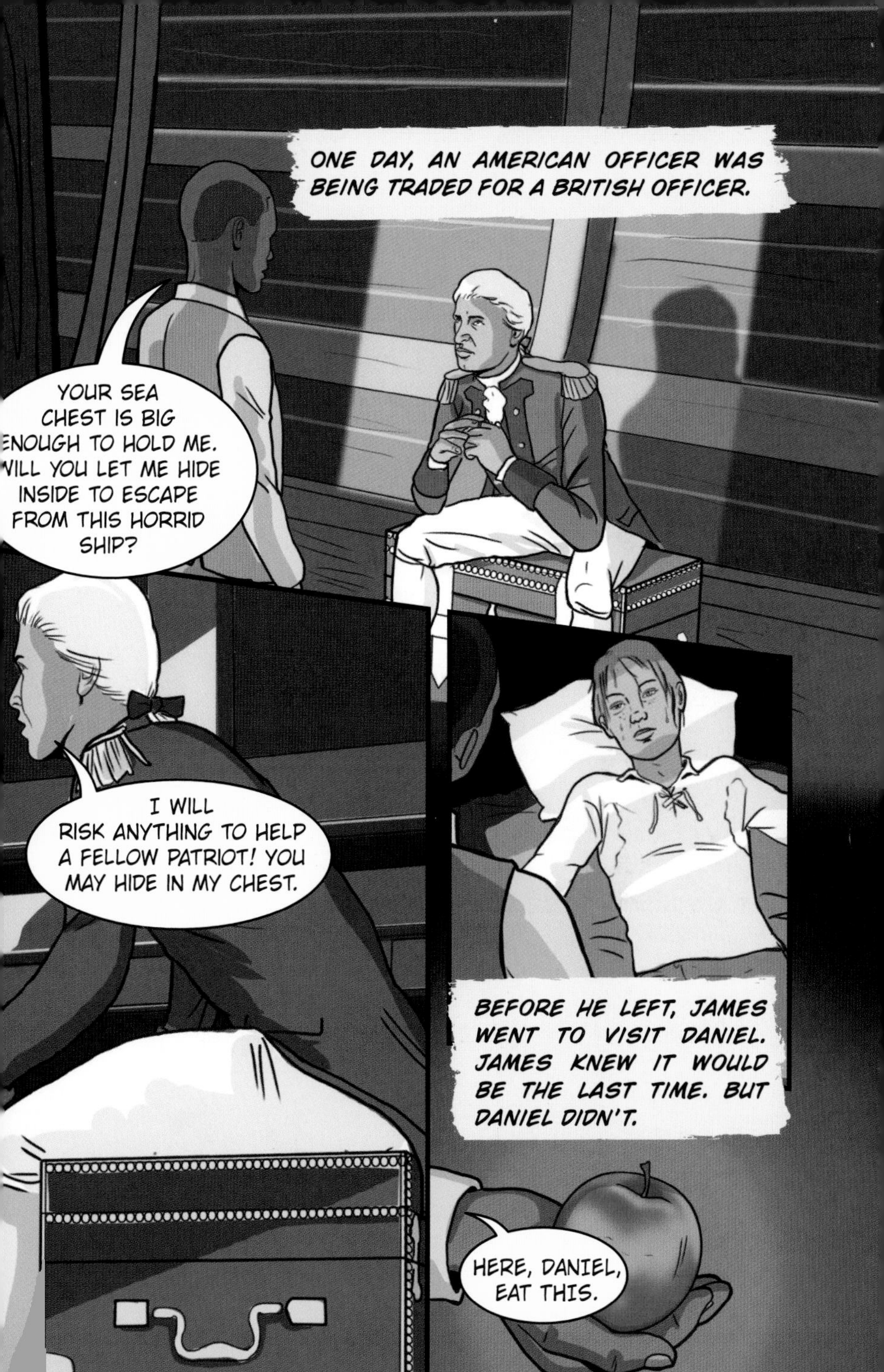
ONE DAY, AN AMERICAN OFFICER WAS BEING TRADED FOR A BRITISH OFFICER.
YOUR SEA CHEST IS BIG ENOUGH TO HOLD ME. WILL YOU LET ME HIDE INSIDE TO ESCAPE FROM THIS HORRID SHIP?
I WILL RISK ANYTHING TO HELP A FELLOW PATRIOT! YOU MAY HIDE IN MY CHEST.
BEFORE HE LEFT, JAMES WENT TO VISIT DANIEL. JAMES KNEW IT WOULD BE THE LAST TIME. BUT DANIEL DIDN'T.
HERE, DANIEL, EAT THIS.

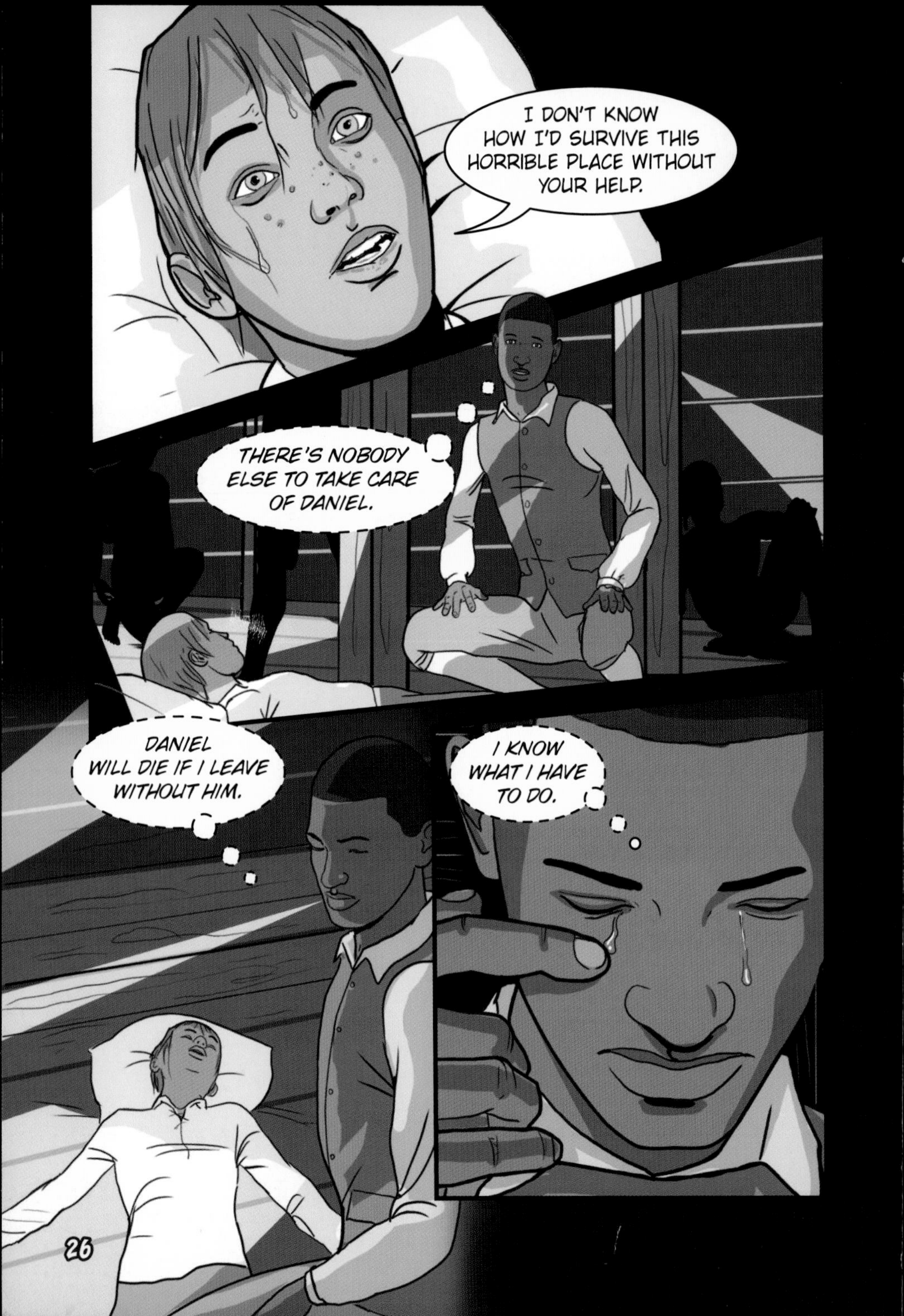
I DON'T KNOW HOW I'D SURVIVE THIS HORRIBLE PLACE WITHOUT YOUR HELP.
THERE'S NOBODY ELSE TO TAKE CARE OF DANIEL.
DANIEL WILL DIE IF I LEAVE WITHOUT HIM.
I KNOW WHAT I HAVE TO DO.

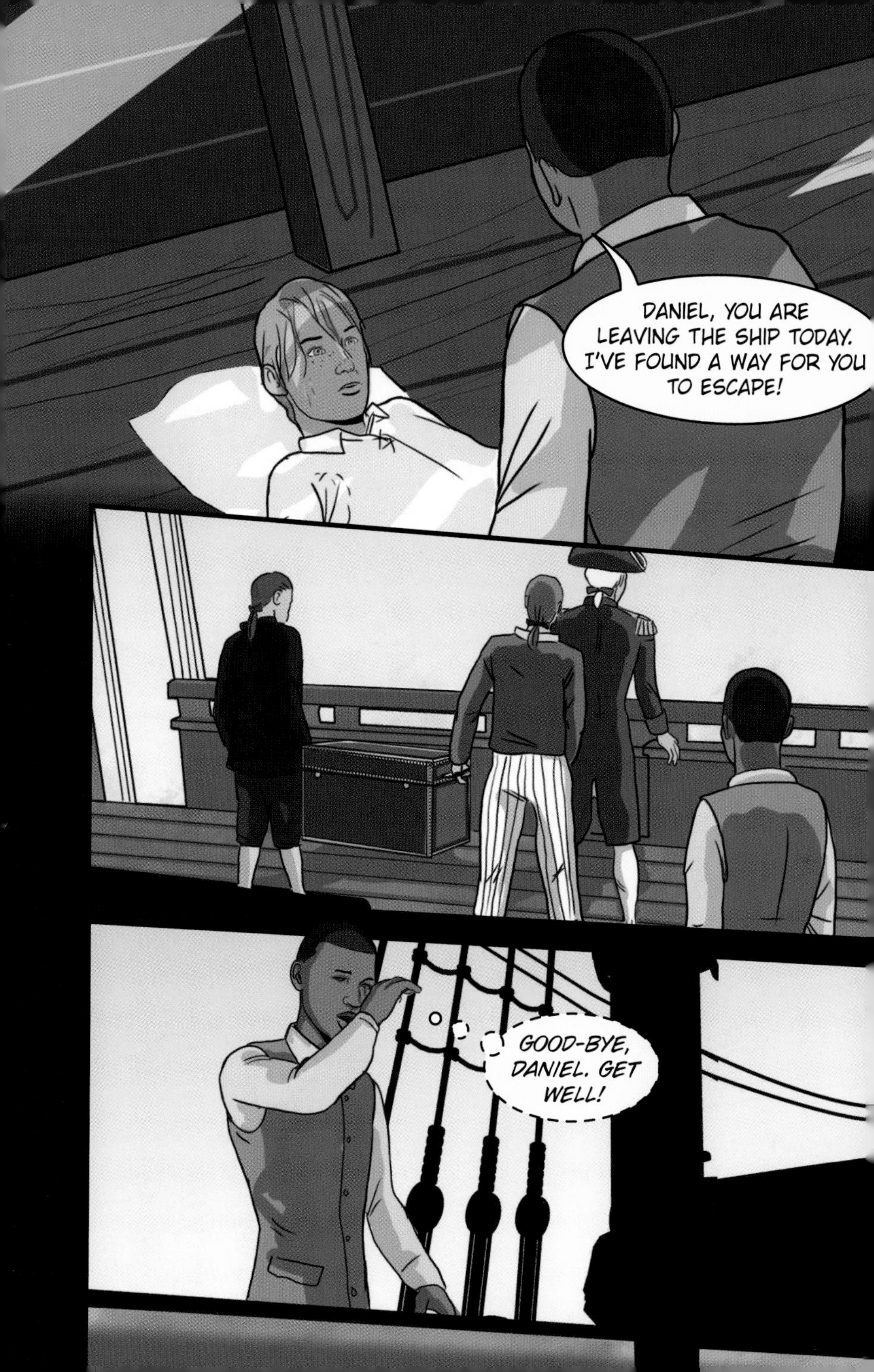
DANIEL, YOU ARE LEAVING THE SHIP TODAY. I'VE FOUND A WAY FOR YOU TO ESCAPE!
GOOD-BYE, DANIEL. GET WELL!

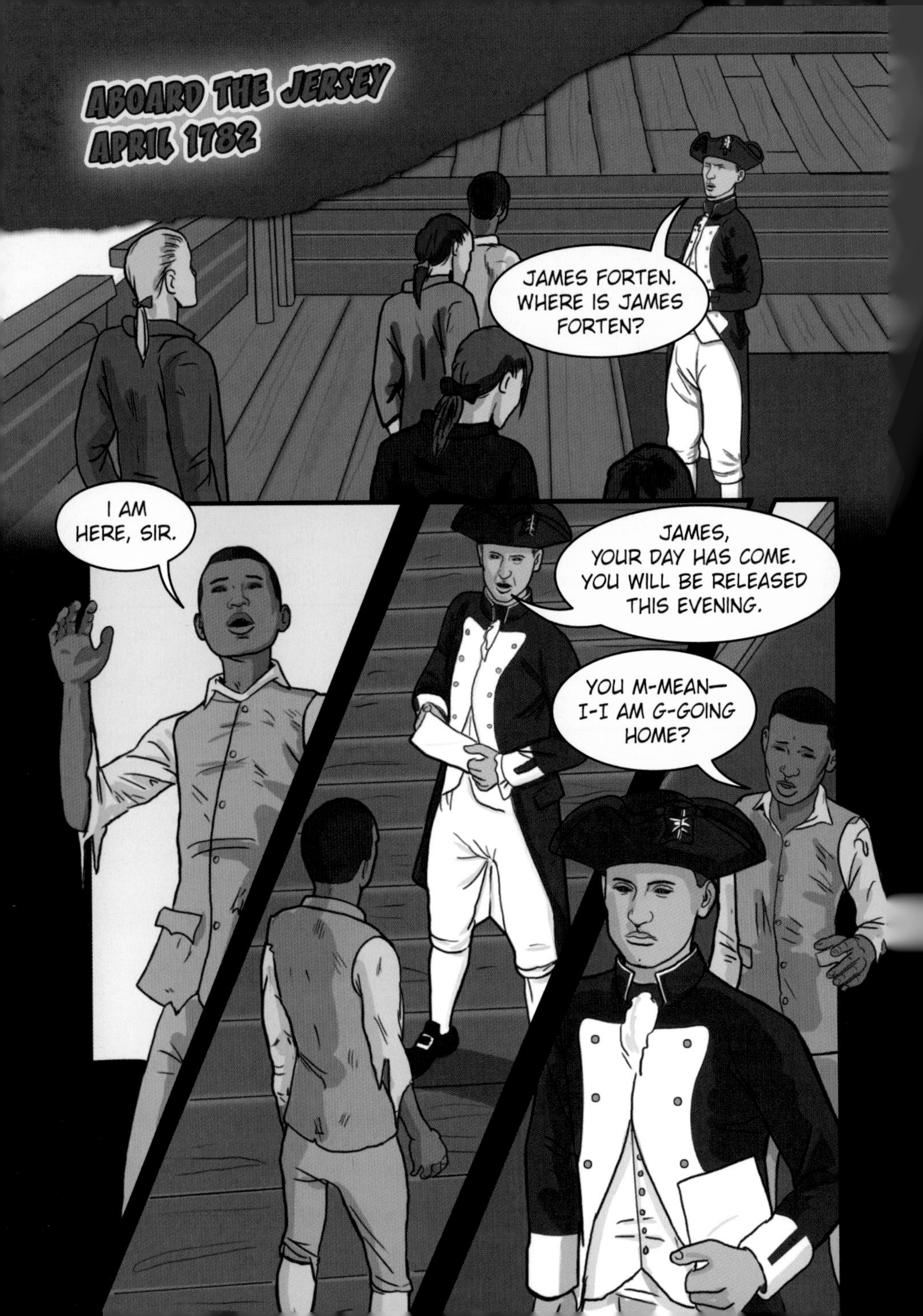
ABOARD THE JERSEY
APRIL 1782
JAMES FORTEN. WHERE IS JAMES FORTEN?
I AM HERE, SIR.
JAMES, YOUR DAY HAS COME. YOU WILL BE RELEASED THIS EVENING.
YOU M-MEAN— I-I AM G-GOING HOME?

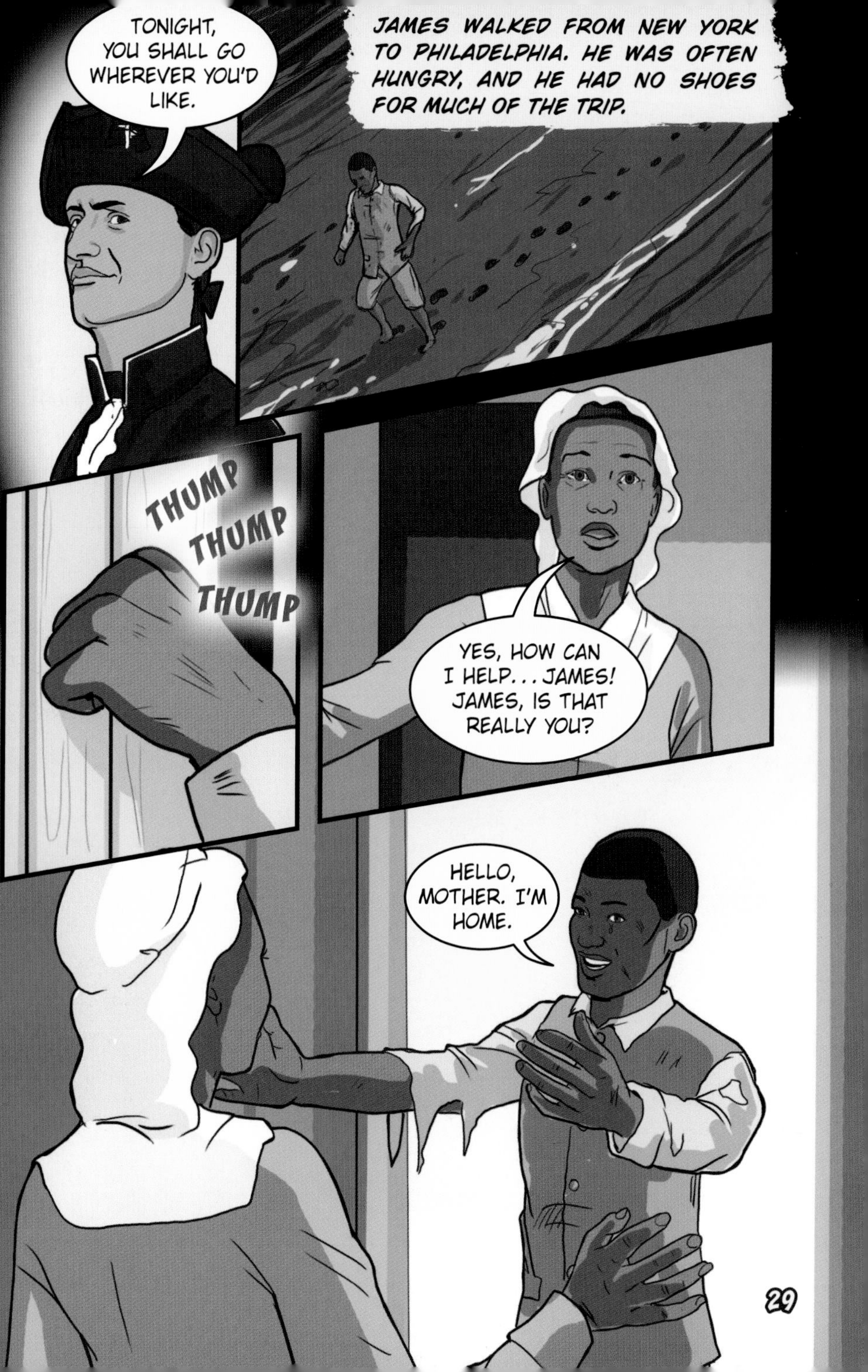
TONIGHT, YOU SHALL GO WHEREVER YOU'D LIKE.
JAMES WALKED FROM NEW YORK TO PHILADELPHIA. HE WAS OFTEN HUNGRY, AND HE HAD NO SHOES FOR MUCH OF THE TRIP.
THUMP THUMP THUMP
YES, HOW CAN I HELP... JAMES! JAMES, IS THAT REALLY YOU?
HELLO, MOTHER. I'M HOME.

AFTERWORD

AFTER JAMES LEFT THE *AMPHION*, HE NEVER SAW CAPTAIN BAZELY OR HENRY AGAIN. JAMES LATER SPOKE ABOUT HIS EXPERIENCE: "THUS . . . DID A GAME OF MARBLES SAVE [ME] FROM A LIFE OF . . . SERVITUDE."

FELLOW PRISONER DANIEL BREWTON SURVIVED. HE NEVER FORGOT JAMES FORTEN'S KINDNESS IN HELPING HIM ESCAPE FROM THE *JERSEY*. DANIEL KNEW THAT JAMES HAD SAVED HIS LIFE. THE TWO MEN BECAME LIFELONG FRIENDS.

AFTER THE WAR, JAMES FORTEN EVENTUALLY RETURNED TO THE SAILMAKING SHOP WHERE HIS FATHER HAD WORKED. BY THE AGE OF 32, JAMES OWNED THE SHOP. HE EMPLOYED 40 MEN, BOTH WHITE AND BLACK. HE BECAME ONE OF THE WEALTHIEST MEN IN PHILADELPHIA.

JAMES BELIEVED THAT ALL BLACK AMERICANS WERE ENTITLED TO THE SAME RIGHTS ENJOYED BY WHITE CITIZENS. HE WAS ACTIVE IN THE ANTISLAVERY MOVEMENT AND HELPED FUND THE FAMOUS ABOLITIONIST NEWSPAPER THE *LIBERATOR*. JAMES FORTEN DIED ON MARCH 4, 1842. MORE THAN 3,000 PEOPLE, BOTH BLACK AND WHITE, ATTENDED HIS FUNERAL.

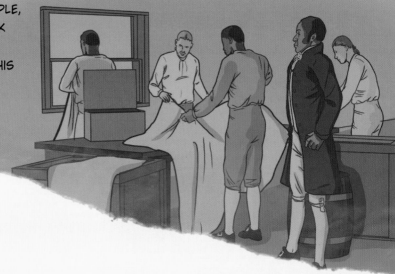

FURTHER READING AND WEBSITES

ALPHIN, ELAINE MARIE, AND ARTHUR B. ALPHIN. *I HAVE NOT YET BEGUN TO FIGHT: A STORY ABOUT JOHN PAUL JONES.* MINNEAPOLIS: MILLBROOK PRESS, 2004.

AMERICA'S STORY FROM AMERICA'S LIBRARY: REVOLUTIONARY PERIOD
HTTP://WWW.AMERICASLIBRARY.GOV/JB/REVOLUT/JB_REVOLUT_SUBJ
.HTML

AMSTEL, MARSHA. *THE HORSE-RIDING ADVENTURE OF SYBIL LUDINGTON, REVOLUTIONARY WAR MESSENGER.* MINNEAPOLIS: GRAPHIC UNIVERSE, 2011.

FIGLEY, MARTY RHODES. *JOHN GREENWOOD'S JOURNEY TO BUNKER HILL.* MINNEAPOLIS: MILLBROOK PRESS, 2011.

HASKINS, JIM. *BLACK STARS OF COLONIAL TIMES AND THE REVOLUTIONARY WAR: AFRICAN AMERICANS WHO LIVED THEIR DREAMS.* NEW YORK: JOSSEY-BASS, 2002.

HAUGEN, DAVID, ED. *VOICES OF THE REVOLUTIONARY WAR: SOLDIERS.* SAN DIEGO: BLACKBIRCH PRESS, 2004.

HISTORICAL MARKERS. EXPLORE PENNSYLVANIA HISTORY
HTTP://EXPLOREPAHISTORY.COM/HMARKER.PHP?MARKERID=870

JAMES FORTEN. BLACK INVENTOR ONLINE MUSEUM
HTTP://WWW.BLACKINVENTOR.COM/PAGES/JAMES-FORTEN.HTML

KREBS, LAURIE. *A DAY IN THE LIFE OF A COLONIAL SAILMAKER.* NEW YORK: POWERKIDS PRESS, 2004.

MILLER, BRANDON MARIE. *GROWING UP IN REVOLUTION AND THE NEW NATION 1775–1800.* MINNEAPOLIS: LERNER PUBLICATIONS COMPANY, 2003.

ROOP, PETER, AND CONNIE ROOP. *THE TOP-SECRET ADVENTURE OF JOHN DARRAGH, REVOLUTIONARY WAR SPY.* MINNEAPOLIS: GRAPHIC UNIVERSE, 2011.

ABOUT THE AUTHOR

MARTY RHODES FIGLEY LIVES IN ANNANDALE, VIRGINIA, WITH HER HUSBAND AND AIREDALE TERRIER, SCARLETT. SHE ENJOYS PLAYING THE ROLE OF "HISTORY DETECTIVE" AS SHE DOES THE RESEARCH FOR HER HISTORICALLY BASED CHILDREN'S BOOKS. MARTY LOVES TO DELVE INTO OLD BOOKS, LETTERS, AND NEWSPAPERS; VISIT MUSEUMS; AND EXPLORE FAMOUS HISTORICAL SITES.

ABOUT THE ADAPTER

AMANDA DOERING TOURVILLE HAS WRITTEN MORE THAN 40 BOOKS FOR CHILDREN. TOURVILLE IS GREATLY HONORED TO WRITE FOR YOUNG PEOPLE AND HOPES THAT THEY WILL LEARN TO LOVE READING AND LEARNING AS MUCH AS SHE DOES. WHEN NOT WRITING, TOURVILLE ENJOYS TRAVELING, PHOTOGRAPHY, AND HIKING. SHE LIVES IN MINNESOTA WITH HER HUSBAND AND GUINEA PIG.

ABOUT THE ILLUSTRATORS

TED HAMMOND IS A CANADIAN ARTIST, LIVING AND WORKING JUST OUTSIDE OF TORONTO. HAMMOND HAS CREATED ARTWORK FOR EVERYTHING FROM FANTASY AND COMIC-BOOK ART TO CHILDREN'S MAGAZINES, POSTERS, AND BOOK ILLUSTRATION.

RICHARD CARBAJAL HAS A BROAD SPECTRUM OF ILLUSTRATIVE SPECIALTIES. HIS BACKGROUND HAS FOCUSED ON LARGE-SCALE INSTALLATIONS AND SCENERY. CARBAJAL RECENTLY HAS EXPANDED INTO THE BOOK PUBLISHING AND ADVERTISING MARKETS.

Text copyright © 2011 by Lerner Publishing Group, Inc.
Illustrations © 2011 by Lerner Publishing Group, Inc.

Graphic Universe™ is a trademark of Lerner Publishing Group, Inc.

Graphic Universe™
A division of Lerner Publishing Group, Inc.
241 First Avenue North
Minneapolis, MN 55401 USA

For reading levels and more information, look up this title at www.lernerbooks.com.

Figley, Marty Rhodes, 1948–
    The prison-ship adventure of James Forten, Revolutionary War captive / by Marty Rhodes Figley; adapted by Amanda Doering Tourville; illustrated by Ted Hammond and Richard Carbajal.
        p.   cm. — (History's kid heroes)
    Summary: In 1781, fifteen-year-old James Forten, a free African American from Philadelphia, is proud to be fighting for the American colonies, but when the British capture the ship on which he serves he fears for both his life and his freedom.
    Includes bibliographical references.
    ISBN: 978-0-7613-6183-1 (lib. bdg. : alk. paper) ISBN: 978-0-7613-7182-3 (EB pdf) 1. Forten, James, 1766–1842—Juvenile fiction. 2. Graphic novels. [1. Graphic novels. 2. Forten, James, 1766–1842—Fiction. 3. African Americans—Fiction. 4. Prisoners—Fiction. 5. United States—History—Revolution, 1775–1783—Fiction.] I. Tourville, Amanda Doering. II. Hammond, Ted, ill. III. Carbajal, Richard, ill. IV. Title.
PZ7.7.T68Pri 2011
973.3'71—dc22   2010035204

Manufactured in the United States of America
5-47265-11498-2/19/2019